PUFFIN BOOKS

PUFFIN BOOKS

Published by the Penguin Group

Penguin Books Ltd, 80 Strand, London WC2R ORL, England

Penguin Group (USA) Inc., 375 Hudson Street, New York, New York 10014, USA

Penguin Group (Canada), 90 Eglinton Avenue East, Suite 700, Toronto, Ontario, Canada M4P 2Y3
(a division of Pearson Penguin Canada Inc.)

Penguin Ireland, 25 St Stephen's Green, Dublin 2, Ireland (a division of Penguin Books Ltd)

Penguin Group (Australia), 250 Camberwell Road, Camberwell, Victoria 3124, Australia
(a division of Pearson Australia Group Pty Ltd)

Penguin Books India Pvt Ltd, 11 Community Centre, Panchsheel Park, New Delhi – 110 017, India

Penguin Group (NZ), 67 Apollo Drive, Rosedale, North Shore 0632, New Zealand
(a division of Pearson New Zealand Ltd)

Penguin Books (South Africa) (Pty) Ltd, 24 Sturdee Avenue, Rosebank, Johannesburg 2196, South Africa

Penguin Books Ltd, Registered Offices: 80 Strand, London WC2R ORL, England

puffinbooks.com

Published in the US by Disney Press, an imprint of Disney Book Group 2010
First published in the UK by Puffin Books 2010

2

Copyright © 2010 Disney Enterprises, Inc.
All rights reserved

Book design by Alfred Giuliani

Set in Filosofia
Made and printed in England by Clays Ltd, St Ives plc

British Library Cataloguing in Publication Data
A CIP catalogue record for this book is available from the British Library

ISBN: 978-0-141-33046-4

www.greenpenguin.co.uk

Penguin Books is committed to a sustainable future
for our business, our readers and our planet.
The book in your hands is made from paper
certified by the Forest Stewardship Council.

Adapted by
T. T. SUTHERLAND

Based on the screenplay by
LINDA WOOLVERTON

Produced by
RICHARD D. ZANUCK, JOE ROTH, SUZANNE TODD *and* **JENNIFER TODD**

Directed by
TIM BURTON

PUFFIN

PROLOGUE

Allison Kingsleigh started awake.

Her heart was pounding. The room around her was dark. The only glimmers of light slipped under the door from the lamps in the hall outside.

She'd had the dream again. It was the same every time.

The tiny nine-year-old pushed back her heavy bedcovers. She shivered as her bare feet hit the cold wooden floor. Sounds echoed from downstairs—the strong, comforting voice of her father and the answering guffaws of his friends in the study.

Pale lace curtains fluttered at her window as Alice pulled open the bedroom door. She crept down the hall, a ghostly figure in her white nightgown. A floorboard creaked underneath her as she passed her mother's room.

Alice froze, waiting for a stern word to send her back to bed.

Silence. Another roar of laughter from the men downstairs. Either her mother was asleep already— or pretending to be.

As Alice hurried down the long staircase, the smooth wood of the banister felt like polished bronze under her small hands. She stopped in the doorway of the study, transfixed by the sight of her father.

Charles Kingsleigh stood before the window, lit by the glow of firelight. A circle of men sat listening to him, captured by his ardor the way Alice usually was. He spoke passionately of his new grand idea.

Alice didn't understand it, but she knew if her father believed in it, it must be something wonderful.

Peering around the door, she recognized one of the faces in the crowd. It was Lord Ascot, a dour, aristocratic man with none of her father's energy or life. Lord Ascot's son, Hamish, was a pasty, stuck-up little boy with no sense of humor. Alice thought he was rather horrible, but she tried to be nice to him. She thought she might be horrible, too, if she had parents like Lord and Lady Ascot.

Instead she had her father, who understood her completely. Alice wrapped her hands around the doorknob and leaned on the solid wooden door, waiting for him to notice her.

"Charles," said Lord Ascot, "you have finally lost your senses."

"This venture is impossible," agreed another man, his mustache twitching.

Charles Kingsleigh smiled a grin that made Alice

feel warm inside. How could anyone disagree with him about anything?

"For some," Alice's father said. "Gentlemen, the only way to achieve the impossible is to believe it is possible."

Alice pondered this.

"That kind of thinking could ruin you," said a man in an ill-fitting black suit, shaking his head.

"I'm willing to take that chance," Charles said passionately. "Imagine trading posts in Rangoon, Bangkok, Jakarta . . ."

He waved his arms, imagining the exotic faraway ports, and his gaze drifted across the room and fell on Alice. Immediately he stopped speaking and crossed the room to her. The other men turned and saw the tiny blond child standing at the door in her nightgown. Alice's father crouched beside her and put his warm hands on her trembling shoulders.

"The nightmare again?" he asked kindly.

Alice nodded, thinking of an immaterial cat and a talking hare. Charles took one of her hands in his and turned to his guests.

"I won't be long," he said.

Alice leaned on his shoulder as he carried her up the long staircase. Her mother would have been scandalized if Alice had shown up in the middle of one of her parties. She would have sent her straight back to bed on her own. But Father understood. He always understood, and he was always there for her.

Charles tucked the bedclothes around Alice again and sat down on the bed beside her.

"Tell me about it," he said, patting her hand.

"I'm falling down a dark hole," Alice said, "and then I see strange creatures. . . ." She faltered. It all sounded too peculiar to believe, but her father listened with a serious, attentive expression on his face.

"What kind of creatures?" he asked.

"Well, there's a dodo bird," said Alice, "a rabbit in a waistcoat, a smiling cat—"

"I didn't know cats could smile," her father said.

"Neither did I," said Alice, but she could see the smiling cat in her head as clear as day, as well as the smile left behind when the rest of the cat disappeared. She shivered. It was so very odd. "Oh, and there's a blue caterpillar," she said, remembering the large puffy mushroom it sat on.

"Blue caterpillar," Charles said gravely. "Hmmm."

Alice gave him a worried look. "Do you think I've gone round the bend?"

Her father felt her forehead, looking just like their family doctor when he was checking for a fever. He made the doctor's "bad news" face and said, "I'm afraid so." Alice's eyes widened, but he went on. "You're mad. Bonkers. Off your head. But I'll tell you a secret . . . all the best people are."

He grinned at her, and Alice couldn't help but

smile back. She leaned against him with a little sigh.

"It's only a dream, Alice," he went on. "Nothing can harm you there. But if you get too frightened, you can always wake up. Like this." Suddenly he pinched her arm, not very hard, but it made her shriek with surprise. Giggling, she pinched him back, and he laughed, tousling her hair.

"Exactly," he said. "You see? Nothing to worry about. It's only a dream." He kissed her forehead and fluffed the pillows around her as he stood up.

"Thank you, Father," Alice whispered.

But as she listened to his footsteps going back down the stairs, a shivery feeling ran across her skin.

How could a dream be so very real?

CHAPTER ONE

TEN YEARS LATER

A horse-drawn carriage careened down the road at a full gallop. Outside the carriage windows, the outskirts of London flashed by. Inside the dark, cramped cab, Alice Kingsleigh fidgeted with her dress. She wished she could be out in the sunshine with a book and a kitten, instead of stuck here on her way to a dreary, boring party with a lot of dreary people.

The little girl haunted by her nightmares had grown into a beautiful woman. There was something slightly unusual—and unearthly—about her beauty. Her large hazel eyes seemed to see things differently from other women her age.

Beside her on the carriage seat, Helen Kingsleigh fussed with Alice's hair. Alice's mother could never understand why Alice's wild blond mane was so unmanageable. Long golden curls seemed to escape no matter what Helen did to pin them all back.

Alice twitched grumpily as her mother yanked on a particularly intractable lock of hair.

"Must we go?" Alice asked. "I doubt they'll notice if we never arrive." She yawned hugely. Her body ached with tiredness, and the last thing she wanted to do was make polite conversation for hours.

"They *will* notice," her mother said firmly. She adjusted Alice's long blue skirt and reached to retie her waist sash. Her thin fingers poked probingly at Alice's stomach. Her eyebrows arched in surprise. "Where's your corset?" she asked, scandalized. What was the world coming to? Couldn't the child even dress herself? Dreading the worst, she lifted

Alice's skirt above her ankles and gasped. "And no stockings!"

"I'm against them," Alice said with another yawn.

"But you're not properly dressed!" Helen pointed out. What would the Ascots think?

"Who's to say what is proper?" Alice said, with that maddening streak of impossible logic she'd inherited from her father. "What if it was agreed that 'proper' was wearing a codfish on your head? Would you wear it?"

Helen closed her eyes. "Alice."

"To me a corset is like a codfish," Alice said.

"Please," said her mother. "Not today."

Alice sighed with frustration and turned to look out the window. "Father would have laughed," she muttered. Instantly, she felt a pang of guilt and turned back to her mother's hurt face. "I'm sorry. I'm tired. I didn't sleep well last night."

Her mother patted her hand forgivingly. "Did you have bad dreams again?"

"Only one," Alice said. Caterpillars and March hares and smiling cats flitted through her mind. She shook her head. "It's always the same, ever since I can remember. Do you think that's normal? Don't most people have different dreams?"

She gave her mother a searching look, but Helen was examining Alice's attire again with a thoughtful expression. She had never been as interested in Alice's dreams as Charles was.

"I don't know," Helen said vaguely. She removed a necklace from around her own neck and clasped it around Alice's with nimble fingers. "There! You're beautiful." She patted her daughter's pale cheek gently. "Now, can you manage a smile?"

The horses slowed to a trot as the carriage pulled up the long, sweeping drive in front of the Ascot mansion. Alice's head ached as she followed her mother out to the gardens, where the party was in full swing. Ladies in the newest style of summer dresses swooped about, twittering over the beautiful flowers like flocks of birds. In the near distance, small skiffs drifted lazily on a meandering river. A few guests were playing croquet on the wide great lawn, the colorful balls bright red, yellow, and blue against the neatly trimmed green of the grass.

Alice pressed her hands to her temples as a piece of her dream flashed before her eyes—equally silly-looking and stuffy guests, playing croquet with flamingos for mallets and hedgehogs for croquet balls. She would have laughed, but something about the scene in her mind filled her with dread. There was someone there . . . someone to fear.

She was distracted from the memory by her mother seizing her hand and hurrying her over to the Ascots. "Smile," Helen reminded her under her breath. Alice fixed an unnatural smile on her face as she curtsied to her elegant hosts.

Lord Ascot hadn't changed in ten years; he was still as ramrod stiff and unflappable as ever. His wife was not much better, although her composure seemed to be rattled today. Her face was red with annoyance as she looked Alice up and down. Alice was sure she noticed the missing corset and stockings. It made Alice want to poke out her tongue and then do a cartwheel, just to make sure Lady Ascot was as well and truly scandalized as she always looked.

"At last!" Lady Ascot burst out. "We thought you'd never arrive. Alice, Hamish is waiting to dance with you." She flapped her hands vigorously at Alice. "Go!"

Alice dutifully allowed herself to be shoved away and went looking for boring old Hamish, who also (very unfortunately) had changed very little in ten years.

Behind her, Lady Ascot lowered her voice as she turned to Helen. "You do realize it's well past four!" she scolded. "Now everything will have to be rushed through!"

"I am sorry," Helen said. She knew better than to explain the whole saga of trying to get Alice ready to go.

"Oh, never mind!" Lady Ascot said abruptly and bustled off, her sharp eyes fixed on a teetering tray of tea sandwiches.

Lord Ascot nodded down at Helen Kingsleigh. "Forgive my wife," he said in his stately baritone. "She's been planning this affair for the last twenty years."

Helen smiled back. She was used to Lady Ascot. "If only Charles were here," she said sadly.

Lord Ascot gave a little bow. "My condolences, madam. I think of your husband often. He was truly a man of wisdom. I hope you don't think I have taken advantage of your misfortune," Lord Ascot went on, looking serious.

"Of course not," Helen said, shaking her head. "I'm pleased that you've purchased the company."

There was much more she could say—how much she missed Charles, how often she thought of him, all of the wonderful things he was in addition to wise— but to express oneself in such a manner was not proper, so she kept her answers short and civilized.

The tall aristocrat allowed himself a small smile. "I was a fool for not investing in his mad venture when I had the chance."

Now Helen's smile was quite real. "Charles thought so, too," she teased.

Elsewhere in the garden, Alice had been drawn into a line dance with the Ascots' son, Hamish. They bowed and stepped and crossed and bowed along with the other young people at the party until Alice felt quite ready to scream with boredom.

"Hamish," she said lightly, "do you ever tire of the quadrille?"

Hamish was refined and immaculately dressed, like his parents. He radiated aristocratic arrogance and a sense of entitlement. His hands felt flabby and damp against hers, and he looked down his long nose at her as if he did not understand the question.

"On the contrary," he replied. "I find it invigorating."

His strutting and preening made him look exactly like the peacocks in Holland Park in Kensington. Alice couldn't help laughing. Her golden hair flew out behind her as they spun around.

Hamish's eyebrows knitted together. "Do I amuse you?"

"No," Alice said, her eyes sparkling mischievously. "I had a sudden vision of all the ladies in top hats and the men wearing bonnets."

Hamish didn't even crack a smile. "It would be

best to keep your visions to yourself. When in doubt, remain silent."

Alice had been hearing this advice her entire life, from everyone except her father. Now that he was gone, she felt as if there were no one else like her in the whole world. Her smile faded, and they kept dancing, although Alice had a hard time keeping her mind on the music. Her eyes drifted to the sky where a flock of geese sailed by overhead.

Distracted, she bumped into the dancers in front of them, who whirled around with outraged expressions.

"Pardon us!" Hamish jumped in officiously before Alice could apologize. "Miss Kingsleigh is distracted today." He ushered Alice away from the dancing green with a frown on his face. Alice glanced up at the sky again, but the geese were gone.

"Where is your head?" Hamish snapped at her.

"I was wondering what it would be like to fly,"

Alice said dreamily. Her father used to lift her over his head and whirl her, shrieking with delight, around the room. She imagined it would be something like that.

"Why would you waste your time thinking about such an impossible thing?" Hamish asked.

Alice laughed, a sound like silver bells in the sunlight. "Why wouldn't I?" she answered him. "My father said he sometimes believed in six impossible things before breakfast." She smiled, remembering one morning when she was seven years old. She'd found her father buttering his toast and demanded to know what the six impossible things were that he'd believed in before breakfast that morning.

"Well," her father had said seriously, setting his toast down and folding his hands. "First I believed that there are three little girls living on the moon."

Alice giggled. "That's silly! How would they get there?"

"That was the second thing," her father said. "I believed they flew there on special flying penny-farthing bicycles. It makes sense, when you think about it."

"No!" Alice cried. "Bicycles can't fly!"

"I see you need more practice believing in impossible things," her father said, returning his attention to his morning cup of tea. "I can't possibly tell you the other four if you're going to disbelieve every one. It would undo all my good work this morning."

"Oh, no, please, please," Alice had begged, leaning against his knee and gazing up at him with wide eyes. "Please tell me the rest! I promise I'll believe in them!"

"All right," he'd said, lifting her onto his knee. "If you promise. The third impossible thing I believed is that the moon must be made of scones and clotted cream, or else what would the little girls eat for tea?"

Alice opened her mouth, saw the warning look on his face, and closed it quickly with a snap.

"But then I had to believe that there must be long bridges on the moon, stretching over the seas of clotted cream, so that the girls would have somewhere to ride their bicycles. Otherwise they would sink into the cream and never be seen again!"

"Of course!" Alice said. She counted on her fingers. "That's four. What was the fifth thing?"

"Fifth," said Charles, "I believed that there was a white rabbit with a monocle who led the girls to the moon and back every night."

Alice gasped. "Just like in my dream! Is it the same rabbit?"

"Most likely," her father said gravely. "He's quite busy, this rabbit. He's got a lot to do, and I hear he's frequently late for his appointments."

"He *is*." Alice breathed, round-eyed with awe.

"And the last impossible thing I believed before breakfast," he said, "was that I have the smartest, prettiest, bravest, most well-behaved daughter in all of London."

"That's not impossible!" Alice protested, giggling again.

"Oh, it was by far the most difficult of the six," Charles assured her. "I had to try terribly hard to believe it. It took me ages and ages. My tea had gone quite cold."

"Father, you're teasing me!" Alice said. She poked the satiny waistcoat over his stomach.

"But the good news is that I believed it at last," her father said, hugging her close. "I believed it so well that it came true, and here you are!"

"Very well," seven-year-old Alice had said, snuggling into his chest. "You may eat your breakfast now."

Nearly twenty-year-old Alice laughed again,

remembering her father's stories. She didn't notice the pained expression on Hamish's face. He wished she could be like other Victorian girls: quiet, restrained, predictable. None of this peculiar talk about impossible things and breakfast. He glanced around and saw his mother hovering at the nearby tea table. Lady Ascot waved impatiently, fixing him with a "hurry up" glare.

Ahem. Hamish cleared his throat and turned to look down his nose at Alice again. "Alice, meet me under the gazebo in precisely ten minutes," he said.

Alice gave his retreating back a curious look. She didn't much like being ordered around. *Precisely* ten minutes! And how was she supposed to achieve that *precisely*, without a pocket watch of any sort? A real gentleman would have given her his, but then he wouldn't have been able to glare at it impatiently when she was late.

Amused by her own wayward train of thought,

Alice stepped toward the refreshments table, but found her way blocked by a pair of giggling girls in gaudy pink and green dresses. The Chattaway sisters were notorious gossips, and from the looks on their faces, they were simply bursting to reveal something they shouldn't.

"We have a secret to tell you," Faith said eagerly.

"If you're telling me, then it's not much of a secret," Alice pointed out. She was not particularly fond of gossip herself.

Fiona clutched Faith's arm. "Perhaps we shouldn't."

"We decided we should!" Faith cried, looking betrayed.

"If we tell her, she won't be surprised," Fiona observed. Alice's interest was piqued. The secret involved her? Perhaps she did want to know after all. She enjoyed surprises even less than gossip.

Faith turned to Alice.

"Will you be surprised?" she demanded, clearly wanting the answer to be "yes."

"Not if you tell me," Alice said. "But now you've brought it up; you have to."

"No, we don't," Faith said. She drew herself up huffily.

"In fact, we won't!" Fiona agreed, looking equally indignant.

Alice sighed. Why did the Chattaways have to be so maddening at all the wrong times? Luckily, she had a trick up her sleeve. She folded her arms. "I wonder if your mother knows that you two swim naked in the Havershims' pond."

The sisters gasped simultaneously.

"You wouldn't!" cried Faith.

"Oh, but I would," said Alice. "There's your mother right now." She took a step toward Lady Chattaway, one of the women cooing over the flowers, and Fiona seized her elbow in a panic.

"Hamish is going to ask for your hand!" she blurted out.

Alice stopped dead. She blinked at Fiona and Faith, too astonished to speak. The two girls beamed and giggled, but their smiles fell as a hand landed on each of their shoulders. Alice's older sister Margaret stood behind them, looking very displeased.

"You've ruined the surprise!" she scolded them. With a push, she sent them off toward the river and pulled Alice aside. "I could strangle them!" she whispered, tucking her hand through Alice's arm. "Everyone went to so much effort to keep the secret."

In a daze, Alice glanced around at the other partygoers. Now she spotted how people kept looking at her, then away again quickly. Now she noticed how their whispers stopped suddenly as she passed. Now she saw the half-hidden smiles of glee on most of the women's faces, the knowing looks on the men. She felt a flutter of panic in her chest.

"Does everyone know?" she asked.

"It's why they've all come," Margaret said brightly. "This is your engagement party! Hamish will ask you under the gazebo." Margaret looked as if she couldn't imagine anything more thrilling. "When you say yes—"

Alice interrupted her. "But I don't know if I want to marry him."

Margaret's face was disbelieving. "Who then? You won't do better than a lord." They both looked over at Hamish, who was standing on the outskirts of the party muttering to himself, rehearsing his proposal, Alice realized. As they watched, he blew his nose vigorously, studied the contents of his handkerchief, then folded it and put it back in his pocket. Alice shuddered.

"You'll soon be twenty, Alice," Margaret said in a no-nonsense voice. She patted Alice's pale cheek. "That pretty face won't last forever. You don't want to end up like Aunt Imogene." She nodded at their middle-aged aunt, who was cramming small sweet cakes into her mouth. Imogene's cheeks were covered in a thick layer of rouge and her yellowing white dress was in a style much too young for her.

Margaret turned Alice around to face her. "And you don't want to be a burden on Mother, do you?"

Alice looked down. "No," she said quietly.

"So you will marry Hamish," Margaret said, satisfied. "You will be as happy as I am with Lowell, and your life will be perfect. It's already decided."

Alice felt as if she were suffocating. The weight of everyone watching her, knowing she had no choice, pressed down on her. Would this have happened if Father were still alive? Surely he would never have made her marry Hamish . . . but he was gone, and there was nothing Alice could do about that. She had to marry Hamish.

It's already decided.

She was trapped.

Chapter Two

Lady Ascot suddenly loomed in front of Alice. Her sharp face leaned down, her features pinched.

"Alice dear," she said smoothly, "shall we take a leisurely stroll through the garden? Just you and me?" She seized Alice's elbow and propelled her away from Margaret. Alice cast a pleading look back over her shoulder, but Margaret only smiled and waved. Her face seemed to say: *that's your future mother-in-law! You'd better get used to it!*

Alice was out of breath by the time they entered the maze of rose gardens. Pink, red, and white roses bloomed all around her, filling the air with their sweet perfume. Lady Ascot kept them moving at a fast clip, and Alice wondered what the hurry was. Her long blond hair was coming unpinned. She thought of how Hamish would disapprove and then gave her head a shake to dislodge a few more pins.

Lady Ascot spoke suddenly. "Do you know what I've always dreaded?"

"The decline of the aristocracy?" Alice suggested, but Lady Ascot did not acknowledge the joke. She carried on as if Alice had not spoken.

"Ugly grandchildren," she said, answering her own question. "But you are lovely." She beamed at Alice's porcelain skin, her lustrous hair, her elfin features. "You're bound to produce little . . . *imbeciles!*"

Alice jumped. That wasn't where she'd expected that sentence to go. But then she realized that Lady Ascot had gotten distracted in the middle of her speech. The aristocratic lady had stopped to glare furiously at an innocent-looking bush of beautiful pearly white roses.

The rosebush shook as Lady Ascot tore off one of the roses and peered at it. "The gardeners planted white roses when I *specifically* asked for red!"

A glimmer of a dream-memory tiptoed through Alice's mind. "You could always paint the roses red," she offered.

Lady Ascot gave her a strange look. "What an odd thing to say." She pushed Alice forward again along the neat gravel path. "Come along."

As they hurried forward, Alice lifted her head. Was that . . . *jingling* that she'd heard? It was hard to tell over the incessant sound of Lady Ascot's voice.

"You should know that my son has extremely delicate digestion," she was saying, but Alice missed the rest of the sentence as something large and white darted past them. She whirled around, blinking, but it was gone again.

"Did you see that?" Alice asked.

Lady Ascot looked displeased at the interruption. "See what?"

Alice gazed around at the dark leaves and brightly colored flowers of the rose garden. "It was a rabbit, I think." She felt a strange prickle along her skin.

"Nasty things." Lady Ascot sniffed. "I do enjoy setting the dogs on them. Don't dawdle." She dragged Alice toward the gazebo, but the younger woman didn't notice. She was still looking for the rabbit as Lady Ascot continued her lecture about Hamish's digestion. "If you serve Hamish the wrong foods," his mother said, "he could get a blockage."

This time it was unmistakable. A large white rabbit was just off the path, standing on its hind legs and staring directly at Alice.

And it was most definitely wearing a waistcoat.

Alice blinked. The rabbit darted behind a tree.

"Did you see it that time?" Alice asked.

"See what?" Lady Ascot said again.

"The rabbit!" Alice cried, getting frustrated.

"Don't shout!" Lady Ascot said snootily. "Pay attention. Hamish said you were easily distracted." She patted her forehead with a white silk handkerchief. "What was I saying?"

"Hamish has a blockage," Alice said, edging away. "I couldn't be more interested, but you'll have to excuse me." She dove into the wooded area off the path, escaping Lady Ascot's clutches. For a moment she blundered through a thick cove of trees, but she saw no sign of the white rabbit. She stopped, her mind reeling.

A hand landed on her shoulder, and she jumped. But it was only Aunt Imogene, her bright pink cheeks disturbingly close to Alice's face.

"Aunt Imogene!" Alice said, leaning back a little. "I think I'm going mad. I keep seeing a rabbit in a waistcoat."

"I can't be bothered with your fancy rabbit now," Imogene said, patting her ridiculous curls. "I'm waiting for my fiancé."

This was strange enough to distract Alice from the rabbit for a moment. "You have a fiancé?"

A sudden flash of white darted past her and she whirled around. "There! Did you see it?" she cried. Her gaze searched the tangled shrubbery frantically, but everything was still again.

"He's a prince," Imogene simpered, ignoring Alice's last question to go back to the story of her fiancé. "But, alas, he cannot marry me unless he renounces his throne. It's tragic, isn't it?"

Alice gave her a skeptical look. "Very." Perhaps Imogene had lost *her* mind. She certainly sounded madder than Alice right now. Alice smiled and nodded politely, backing away from her aunt. Imogene had her hands clasped under her chin and was gazing off into the distance, waiting for her imaginary fiancé to appear. Alice was able to duck behind a tree, and she ran right into her sister's husband, Lowell.

To her surprise, Lowell had his arms around a woman and was kissing her passionately. That woman, however, was not his wife, Margaret. Whoever she was, she took one look at Alice, let out a little shriek, and ran off into the woods.

"Lowell?" Alice said disbelievingly.

"Alice," he said, highly flustered. "We were just . . . uh, Hattie's an old friend."

Alice lifted her eyebrows. "I can see you're very close." Not ten minutes earlier, Margaret had been extolling the virtues of married life and explaining how being married to Hamish would make Alice's life as perfect as her own, married to Lowell. Was this what she meant? Did she really have no idea what was happening behind her back? Could Margaret be happy with a man like this?

Lowell adjusted his cravat. His face was bright red.

"Look, you won't mention this to your sister, will you?" he asked.

"I don't know," Alice said, stepping back. She didn't want to cause Margaret pain—but shouldn't she know the truth about her husband? She didn't know what the right thing to do was. "I'm confused. I need time to think."

"Well, think about Margaret," Lowell said, half-pleading, half-commanding. "She would never trust me again. You don't want to ruin her marriage, do you?" He ended with a threatening tone in his voice.

"Me?" Alice protested. "But I'm not the one who's sneaking around behind her back. . . ."

Chapter Two

"*There* you are!" Hamish's voice interrupted. He popped out of the trees and seized Alice's hand. Without a word to Lowell, he dragged her away.

Alice stumbled on the rough ground. It seemed far too soon to find herself standing with Hamish under the statuesque gazebo that adorned the garden. The shadows of the pillars fell on her like prison bars. She shifted uncomfortably, feeling cornered. As she glanced around, she spotted a string quartet discreetly positioned in the shadows. Their bows were already lifted and poised to play . . . just waiting for her to say yes before they added some swelling music to the dramatic moment.

Hamish dropped to one knee. Alice's heart sank with him. She'd been hoping that Margaret was somehow wrong, that this wasn't really about to happen.

"Alice Kingsleigh . . ." he said, taking her hand.

"Hamish," Alice interrupted him.

"What is it?" he asked, frowning.

"You have a caterpillar on your shoulder."

Hamish jerked backward and began frantically brushing at his shoulder, wriggling in disgust.

"Don't hurt it!" Alice cried. She stepped forward and let the caterpillar crawl onto her finger. Then she lifted it gently onto a tree branch.

Hamish curled his lip at her hands as she came back to stand in front of him again. "You'll want to wash that finger," he said, edging away from her. Alice didn't mind. She much preferred it when he wasn't touching her.

Someone cleared her throat nearby, and the two young people in the gazebo glanced around to see Hamish's mother gesturing eagerly at them. In fact, a whole crowd of people was watching them. Alice felt the weight of all their eyes on her, and apparently Hamish did, too, for he blurted out: "Alice Kingsleigh, will you be my wife?"

Chapter Two

The question hung in the air for a long moment.

Unsure of herself, unsure of her future, unsure of her own sanity in that moment, Alice began to stammer. "Well, everyone expects me to . . . and you're a Lord . . . and my face won't last . . . and I don't want to end up like . . . but this is happening so quickly . . . I, I . . . think . . . I . . ."

Something caught her eye.

It was the white rabbit, leaning against a pillar of the gazebo, glaring at her with undisguised impatience.

Maybe she was crazy. But she couldn't exactly *ignore* him.

"I need a moment," she explained, backing away. She seized the skirts of her long dress, turned, and ran.

Cries and murmurs from the crowd bubbled up behind her, but she didn't look back. She ran with her golden hair flying out behind her, chasing the rabbit, just as she had in her dream, over and over again.

They ran across the manicured garden, into a thicket of woods, and out into an open meadow that Alice didn't recognize. Small yellow butterflies darted over the tall grass, and hedgerows rose up along the edges.

Alice ran as fast as she could, but she'd lost sight of the rabbit in the grass. Gasping for breath, she stopped and looked around. She peeked over the hedgerow. The rabbit was nowhere to be found.

Suddenly, a white paw reached up and grabbed her by the ankle. With a quick jerk, it yanked her off her feet. Alice threw out her arms and screamed.

She was falling
    down
        the rabbit hole.

CHAPTER THREE

Alice's screams echoed as she tumbled head over heels down the enormous, dark hole. Her hands reached out, searching for something to stop her fall, and she realized that the walls around her were lined with odd things . . . things you would never expect to find in a rabbit hole. Hanging on the dirt walls were crooked paintings, ancient maps, cracked mirrors, demonic masks, and bookshelves crowded with bizarre paraphernalia.

She grabbed the first thing her hand touched and found herself holding an empty jam jar. Frustrated and terrified, she let that go and grabbed for something else—a crystal ball. Growing frantic, she scrabbled through object after peculiar object, finding herself holding books, more jam jars, a badger claw, a monkey's hand, and finally a human skull. With another shriek, she flung this last terrible thing away from her and kept falling, down and down and down into deeper darkness, where there was no longer anything to hold on to.

Still she fell, as day passed into night, down and down, still falling.

Finally, after what seemed like hours, Alice landed on a hard wooden floor, smacking her head as she hit the ground.

"Ah!" she cried in pain as the wind was knocked out of her. She gasped for air for a moment, then sat up, rubbing the bump on her head.

She was in a circular hall with closed doors all around her. There was something strangely familiar about it, although she couldn't imagine when she would have been in a round room at the bottom of a rabbit hole.

Alice got to her feet and tried one of the doors, but it was locked. She tried the next—and the next—but they were all locked. What was the use of so many doors if you couldn't go through any of them?

Finally she took a step back and glanced around the hall. That's when she noticed a three-legged glass table nearby. Had that been there before? She didn't understand how she could have missed it.

There was a tiny gold key sitting on top of the glass tabletop. Alice picked it up and tried it in a couple of the doors, but it was far too small. She paused and studied the key for a moment, then glanced around at all the doors in the hall, wondering if any of them were small enough for this key.

She spotted a thick velvet curtain between two of the doors and swept it aside, revealing a door much smaller than the others. It was only about two feet high and quite narrow, with a pattern of vines carved into the wood.

Alice crouched to fit the tiny key into the lock of the little door. It fit perfectly. The small door swung open, and she ducked her head to look through to the other side.

It was difficult to see much, but she could tell that beyond the door was a garden with a fountain in the center. She got down on her stomach and tried to squeeze through the doorway, but her shoulders got stuck in the frame, and no matter how she wriggled, she couldn't go through.

With a sigh, she wriggled back into the hall and shut the door again. Stumped, she climbed to her feet and went to put the key back on the table. But to her surprise, there was now a bottle sitting on the glass top of the table. She was *sure* it hadn't been there before. Alice looked around curiously.

The hall looked deserted. Alice squinted at the

bottle. A tiny white label around its neck said: DRINK ME. Yes, that sounds like a great idea, Alice thought. Follow the mysterious instructions of someone you can't see. Drink a mystery potion. What could go wrong?

She removed the top, sniffed the contents of the bottle, and recoiled. It didn't smell appetizing.

Alice looked around the room again. On the other hand, she didn't have a lot of choices. She shrugged. "It's only a dream," she said aloud to herself. A familiar dream . . . although she couldn't remember falling asleep. Maybe in the meadow? Or in the woods on the way to the gazebo? It was all so muddled now. But this had to be a dream. There was nothing real about it. And if it was a dream, then what could happen to her?

Alice poured some of the drink into her mouth, shuddered, and coughed, gagging at the taste. Apparently things could still taste horrible, even in dreams.

She replaced the bottle top and suddenly noticed that the table was getting larger. She frowned at it.

It took her another few moments to realize that the table wasn't growing. She held out her pale hands and stared at them in shock as she got smaller and smaller and smaller. Finally she was two feet tall, surrounded by a puddle of her now-oversize clothes.

Well, that raises some new problems . . . but at least it also solves one, she thought. Wrapping her skirts around her arms to lift them out of the way, Alice flounced over to the small door and tried to open it.

She groaned in dismay. It was locked again! And of course she'd left the key on top of the table. She turned and gazed up at it through the glass tabletop. The key glittered in the dim light, mocking her from far out of reach.

What Alice didn't know was that at that very moment, she was being watched.

A round eye blinked at her through a keyhole.

"You'd think she would remember this from the first time," muttered the eye's owner.

There was a flutter of feathers and some jostling, and a new, smaller eye, this one rimmed in brown fur, replaced the first one at the keyhole. "You've brought the wrong Alice," said this new watcher.

"She's the right one." said another voice behind them, indignantly. "I'm certain of it."

The second eye blinked dubiously.

Alice was now trying to climb the table leg, but she kept getting tangled in her too-big clothes and sliding down. She was starting to think this was impossible. She'd never get back to that key. She'd be stuck, tiny and trapped and tormented by the key just out of reach, until she wasted away and died.

Then she noticed a small box under the table. Now *that* hadn't been there before, either! Alice whirled around and glared at the doors of the hall.

Exasperated, Alice opened the box. Inside was a beautiful little cake with the words EAT ME written on it in ornate pink icing. It was almost too pretty to eat, but again, she didn't have much choice. She considered the cake, then looked up at the key, high above her on the table. It was worth a shot. Of course, she might disappear altogether, but then she'd just wake up from the dream, and that would be all right, too.

Alice took a tiny bite of the cake, and then another.

WHOOSH!

Suddenly she shot upward. She grew and grew at an alarming rate. She reached her normal size, where her clothes fit again . . . and then kept growing. Buttons popped, seams began to strain, and her skirt got shorter—Alice couldn't help thinking how scandalized Lady Ascot would be at the sight of her bare ankles. But then she was distracted by the feeling of her head bumping against the ceiling. What if she kept growing until she filled the whole hall? What would happen then?

To her relief, that was where she stopped. Towering over the table, she bent far down and picked up the small key. It looked no bigger than an eyelash in her giant hand. She sidled across the room, crouched, and put the key into the small door's lock.

"She's the wrong Alice," said the second voice definitively.

"Give her a chance," the third voice insisted.

Alice giggled a little at the thought of trying to fit through the door at her current enormous size. She sat down with the bottle in one hand and the cake in the other. Sipping from one and then nibbling from the other, she managed to shrink and grow and shrink herself down to the perfect size for the door, about two feet tall. Of course, now her clothes were far too big again, but she'd solved one problem.

Dragging her skirts behind her, she ran to the door, unlocked it, and stepped through.

CHAPTER FOUR

The world Alice stepped into was strange and beautiful and unexpected, like a garden glimpsed in a mirror from far away. For some reason she had expected it to be full of flowers—talking flowers with silly personalities. But this garden was brown and tangled instead. Stone statues littered the walkways, many of them broken and overgrown with dead vines. The fountain no longer glittered with sun-speckled water. It was still and empty, covered in a creeping greenish-brown moss.

"*HAAACHOOOOOORRRRRW!*" Something bellow-sneezed behind her. Alice whirled around and saw a green pig dash past, its emerald hooves clattering on the dusty gravel paths. She blinked at its curly, brilliant green tail as it vanished behind a long hedge.

Her eyes fell on a row of flowers, and she jumped. They *did* have human faces—how had she known they would? But these were not the ones she'd expected somehow. These faces were gaunt and haunted, as if the flowers were starving. Their eyes stared blankly past her, and their petals hung limp, with pale, washed-out colors barely visible against the brown and gray backdrop. None of them spoke to her, although a couple let their gaze travel slowly across her face, then drift back down to the ground.

Now that Alice was paying closer attention, she could see living things moving all around her. Up in the air, dragonflies the size of horses were doing battle with horseflies the size of dragons and gnats that were bigger than any animal she'd ever seen.

They swooped and zoomed toward one another, stinging and buzzing angrily. The weak sun, hidden by a haze of gray clouds, barely illuminated the blue-green bodies of the dragonflies and the iridescent wings of all the battling insects.

Alice jumped again as another creature stalked past her—a shabby, thin bird on legs as tall and thin as the stilts little boys played with in the alleys outside her London home. She saw more birds that looked much the same: shoulders hunched, drab feathers falling out, knobbly legs that looked too skinny to support even the bird's thin frame.

"Curiouser and curiouser," Alice muttered. This place was familiar and yet . . . somehow not. It seemed . . . sadder than she had imagined.

"I told you she's the right Alice," a voice said triumphantly.

Alice whirled around. A cluster of the oddest creatures stood behind her, all of them staring at her intently. The speaker was the White Rabbit, who stood with his front paws neatly tucked into his waistcoat. His long ears and wiggly nose twitched as he studied her.

She was getting an equally intense look from the large bird next to the White Rabbit—a dodo bird, if she was not mistaken. He was peering at her through a pair of eyeglasses and leaning on a walking stick.

The rest of the party consisted of one young dormouse in breeches and a pair of very round boys with their arms thrown over each other's shoulders. Words were embroidered on their stiffly starched white collars. One said DEE and the other said DUM.

"I am not convinced," said the Dormouse, shifting back and forth on her paws.

The White Rabbit threw up his hands. "How is that for gratitude!" he cried. "I've been up there for weeks trailing one Alice after the next! I was almost *eaten* by other animals! Can you imagine?

They go about entirely unclothed and they do their . . . *shukm* . . . in public." A full-body shudder rippled through his white fur. "I had to avert my eyes." He touched one paw to his forehead dramatically.

"She doesn't look anything like herself," one of the flowers suddenly offered. A few of the other flowers with human faces perked up a little and squinted at Alice, who felt rather like a specimen under a microscope at this point.

"That's because she's the wrong Alice," the Dormouse said again.

The pair of boys spoke up.

"And if she was, she might be," said the one with Dee on his collar.

"But if she isn't, she ain't," said Dum.

"But if she were so, she would be."

"But she isn't. No-how."

They both shook their round, moonlike faces solemnly.

Alice put her hands on her hips. "How can I be the 'wrong Alice' when it's *my* dream?" she demanded. "And who are *you*, if I may ask?"

One of the round boys seized her hand. "Oh, I'm Tweedledee, and he's Tweedledum," he rattled off quickly.

"Contrariwise," the other piped up, "I'm Tweedledum—he's Tweedledee."

Which didn't give her much of an answer, really.

The Dodo cleared his throat. "We should consult Absolem."

The others all nodded. Even the talking flower's head bobbed up and down. "Exactly," said the flower. "Absolem will know who she is."

Tweedledee offered Alice his arm. "I'll escort you," he offered.

Just as she was about to take it, Tweedledum suddenly seized her elbow and yanked her away. "Hey, it's not being your turn! So unfair!" he insisted.

Tweedledee grabbed her other arm and tried to tug her back to him. "Hey, leave off!" he yelled.

"Let go!" bellowed the other.

Alice thought she might split in two in a minute. She wriggled free and jumped away. "Are they always this way?" she asked the rabbit.

"Family trait," the White Rabbit answered. "You can both escort her," he said firmly to the Tweedles.

Shooting daggers at each other with their eyes, Tweedledee and Tweedledum each took one of Alice's arms and led her forward. The Dormouse, the Dodo, and the White Rabbit followed close behind.

As they walked through the overgrown garden, Alice could hear the talking flowers whispering about her whenever they passed by.

"It can't be her," murmured a glum-looking daisy.

"She looks nothing like Alice," agreed a drooping tiger lily.

"She is not even wearing the right dress," complained one of the violets.

Alice peered at the tiger lily as they hurried by. It couldn't look familiar . . . how silly! All tiger lilies looked the same, surely. And yet there was something about this one, as if they'd met before. How peculiar this dream was getting!

"Who is this Absolem?" Alice asked her companions. She couldn't remember dreaming about an "Absolem" before.

"He's wise," said the White Rabbit. "He's absolute."

"He's Absolem," the Tweedles added in unison, as if that should answer the question. Alice realized she wasn't going to get much more useful information out of them. She'd have to wait until they reached this wise old Absolem.

She blinked, then blinked again. The garden path sloped down a little hill, and slowly—so slowly that at first she hadn't noticed it—they were surrounded by a strange mist. Through the mist she could see that they were wandering into a tall forest, but the trees were not by any means ordinary. Their trunks were fat and pale, and when Alice looked up to find branches, she saw instead a flat brownish gray canopy extending out from the top of the trunk in an unbroken, round circle.

"Oh!" she gasped softly. They weren't trees . . . they were mushrooms! She was standing in a forest of tall mushrooms, many of them towering high above her head. The earth was spongy and squishy and dark under her shoes.

"Who are you?" intoned a deep voice.

Alice's eyes traveled up the nearest trunk—up and up and up to where the mist was rising in a steady plume. It wasn't an ordinary mist. It was the smoke from a hookah. And that hookah was currently being smoked by a very large blue caterpillar.

A shiver danced across Alice's skin. She *did*

remember something about a blue caterpillar.
But before she could fit the pieces of her memory
together, the White Rabbit pushed her toward the
mushroom.

"Um," Alice stammered. "Absolem?"

The Caterpillar writhed a little, looking
displeased. "You're not Absolem," it pointed
out. "*I'm* Absolem. The question is . . . who are
YOU?"

He inhaled deeply, then puffed a series of smoke
rings in her face. Alice coughed and tried to wave the
smoke away.

"Alice," she answered when she could breathe
again.

"We shall see," the Caterpillar responded
skeptically.

"What do you mean by that?" Alice demanded.
All this nonsense about being the wrong Alice was
starting to annoy her. "I ought to know who I am!"

"Yes, you ought," said the Caterpillar with a disapproving look. "Stupid girl. Unroll the Oraculum," he added commandingly.

The White Rabbit hopped over to a nearby toadstool, only as high as Alice's shoulders. He bounced up on his strong back paws and grabbed the ancient parchment lying rolled up on top of it. With a dramatic flourish, he unrolled it.

"The Oraculum," he announced. "Being a Calendrical Compendium of Underland."

Alice peered over his shoulder. It was the oddest scroll. It looked nothing like her neat schoolbooks with their even rows of dates and boring historical facts. But it was clearly a timeline, with important events marked for each day. Every day had a title, but every day also had an odd little illustration next to it . . . and some of them were moving!

"It's a calendar," Alice guessed.

"Compendium," the Caterpillar corrected her.

"It tells of each and every day since the Beginning."

"Today is Griblig Day in the time of the Red Queen," explained the White Rabbit. He pointed with one paw at the illustration for "Griblig Day."

To Alice's surprise, the illustration showed her, the White Rabbit, and all the others peering at the Oraculum—exactly the way they were peering at it that very moment!

Well, that's odd, she thought. More than odd, it's curious. And it makes me curious. How did the parchment know what was going to happen before it happened?

"Show her the Frabjous Day," said the Caterpillar. Its long blue coils rippled as it went back to smoking the hookah.

The White Rabbit flipped ahead in the scroll, turning the rolls on either side to advance into the future. Tweedledee was too impatient to wait. He was dancing on his small round feet.

"Oh yeah, Frabjous being the day you slay the Jabberwocky," he told Alice.

"Sorry?" she said. "Slay a . . . what?"

He pointed at the Oraculum, and Alice turned slowly to see the illustration on "Frabjous Day." It was one of the moving pictures—unfortunately, since the thing moving in it was one of the most horrible creatures Alice had ever seen. It was as tall as a giraffe with reptilian wings, scales, long sharp claws, a pronged tail, and a vest. Not to mention its enormous gnashing teeth and wide, flaming eyes.

In the picture, the Jabberwocky hissed furiously at a female knight with long blond hair, wearing chain mail, and carrying a shining sword. They fought, blade clashing against claws and scales, and the Jabberwocky shrieked with anger.

Tweedledum's pudgy finger poked into her view, tapping the illustration of the knight. "Oh, yeah, that being you there with the Vorpal Sword."

"No other swords can kill the Jabberwocky," said Tweedledee. "No-how."

"If it ain't Vorpal, he ain't dead," said Tweedledum.

Alice stared at the image, transfixed. That *couldn't* be her. She'd never worn chain mail in her life! Let alone lifted a sword! She couldn't even imagine battling a giant monster like that!

The knight in the picture swung her sword, turning her face toward the readers of the scroll. Alice gasped.

It *was* her. Most unmistakably. And she had bloodlust in her eyes.

CHAPTER FIVE

lice backed away from the Oraculum, shaking her head.

"That's not me," she said. She refused to believe it. It was more impossible than any of the impossible things her father had ever believed before breakfast.

"I know!" the Dormouse agreed. She flapped her furry hands at the White Rabbit, as if to hurry him along.

The White Rabbit sighed. "Resolve this for us, Absolem," he pleaded, twitching his ears at the blue Caterpillar. "Is she the right Alice?"

The Caterpillar peered over the top of his mushroom. He looked Alice in the eye and thought for a long, tense moment.

"Not hardly," he said at last. Smoke billowed out of his hookah, obliterating him from view.

Pandemonium broke out among the creatures on the ground.

"I told you!" the Dormouse cried.

"Oh, dear!" squealed the White Rabbit, throwing up his paws. He looked horribly dismayed, and for a moment Alice felt quite bad for being so very much the "wrong" Alice.

"I said so!" said Tweedledum.

"*I* said so," said Tweedledee.

"Contrariwise, you said she might be," snapped his brother.

"No, *you* said she would be if she *was*," shouted Tweedledee.

"Little imposter!" cried the Dodo. "Pretending

to be Alice! She should be ashamed!"

All of them glared at Alice as if everything was somehow her fault.

"I'm sorry!" Alice protested. "I don't mean to be the wrong Alice!" She really thought this was all rather unfair. "Wait, this is *my* dream," she remembered. "I'm going to wake up now, and you'll all disappear." Wrong Alice, indeed!

She closed her eyes and firmly pinched herself, the way her father had shown her. After a moment, she opened her eyes again.

The creatures were all still there staring at her, with the pale mist-wreathed trunks of the mushroom forest behind them.

She pinched herself again, harder this time.

The animals just looked at her. Nobody had the good manners to disappear.

"That's odd," Alice muttered. "Pinching usually does the trick." She frowned at the creatures in puzzlement.

The Dormouse pulled a long, sharp hatpin from the scabbard hanging on her breeches. "I could stick you if that would help," she offered.

Alice considered the idea for a moment. "It might, actually," she said. "Thank you."

"My pleasure," said the Dormouse, a little too gleefully. She scampered over and stabbed Alice in the ankle with relish.

"Argh!" Alice shrieked, grabbing for her foot. That hurt more than a pinch—and it *still* didn't work. This was a horrible dream!

And it promptly got much worse. A thunderous roar echoed through the mushroom forest, shaking the soggy ground beneath them. Alice screamed as something came crashing through a high wall nearby. For a terrifying moment, she thought it was the Jabberwocky.

But then she realized that this new beast was furry, not scaly. It had the head of a rabid bulldog and was oozing drool from its squashed muzzle. Its fur was caked with blood and filth. Its teeth looked like shark's teeth, broken and stained with blood. A foul stench wafted from its huge furry body.

It might not be the Jabberwocky, but it was equally bloodcurdling!

"*Bandersnatch!*" yowled Tweedledee.

"Eeeeeeeeeeeeeeeeeeeeeeeee!" shrieked Tweedledum. "It's so *frumious!*"

Everyone scattered, fleeing for their lives. Alice covered her head and ran back toward the garden. Her heart pounded madly in her chest. She did not want to be eaten, even in a dream.

All throughout the garden and the mushroom forest, animals were fleeing in terror. But many of them found themselves running into the arms of an equally dangerous foe. Tall Red Knights intercepted them, waving swords and shouting orders. The

White Rabbit spotted the crest on their armor—a heart in flames—the Red Queen's crest. The White Rabbit bolted through a hedge, hoping to escape.

Ahead of him, a pig and a flamingo were seized by rough, armor-clad arms and flung into a caged wagon. As the rabbit darted under a low branch, he saw the Dodo slip through the circle and escape.

Unfortunately, the White Rabbit was not so lucky.

A knight grabbed his leg and lifted him into the air. The White Rabbit flailed angrily, waving his paws. "Unhand me!" he shouted. "I do not enjoy being—"

The rest of his sentence was muffled as he was tossed into the caged wagon with the other animals.

Alice saw none of this; she was still racing down a garden path, feeling the hot, smelly breath of the Bandersnatch close on her heels. The ground shook as his meaty paws thundered behind her.

Suddenly, Alice skidded to a stop. "Wait," she said. "It's only a dream!" For a moment the fear had made her forget. She nearly laughed. "Nothing can hurt me," she reminded herself. Crossing her arms, she turned to face the Bandersnatch.

Not far away, the Dormouse watched from behind a tree. She pressed her paws to her face in disbelief. "What is she *doing*?" she whispered.

The Bandersnatch loomed over Alice. Drool dripped from its muzzle onto her shoes as it opened its mouth wide to devour her.

"Can't hurt me," Alice said defiantly. This was an *awfully* realistic dream. But it had to be a dream. None of this could possibly be real. "Can't hurt me," she said again, a little less confidently this time.

"Run, you great lug!" the Dormouse screamed. With a groan of despair, the tiny mouse darted out from behind the tree and leaped onto the Bandersnatch. She pulled herself up, paw over paw, to its shoulder and drove her hatpin straight into its wild, rolling eye.

"RRROOOOOOOWWWWRRRRRR!" the Bandersnatch bellowed in pain. It thrashed and kicked furiously. The Dormouse struggled to pull out the hatpin . . . but the whole eye popped out!

The Bandersnatch's howls increased in fury. It whipped around, lashed out, and raked Alice's arm with its long claws.

"Ow!" Alice shrieked. She'd had enough of testing this dream. She turned and ran for her life.

Back in the mushroom forest, the Oraculum lay forgotten and unattended on the ground, where it had been dropped in the mad stampede to escape the Bandersnatch. A long, quiet moment passed, and then a grim-looking man stepped out of the mist and stared down at it. A flaming red birthmark covered half his face and hands, and he also wore the crest of the Red Queen. He picked up the Oraculum and studied the page it was open to.

An alarmed look flitted across his face. He glanced around surreptitiously, tucked the scroll into his saddlebag, and rode away.

The Tweedles suddenly appeared, running one on either side of Alice. They pointed at the path up ahead, where it diverged in two directions. A road sign indicated that one direction led to "QUEAST" and the other led to "SNUD," which really told Alice nothing.

"This way!" Tweedledum shouted. "East to Queast!"

"No!" Tweedledee bellowed. "South to Snud!"

Each grabbed an arm and tried to pull her down his chosen path. Alice felt as if she were being ripped in two. She didn't care which way she went— she just wanted to get away!

An ear-splitting screech rang out from above. The Tweedles froze in terror as an enormous bird landed in front of them. It had the terrifying death-dealing beak of an eagle and the long towering legs of an ostrich. Blood dripped from its mouth as it clattered its beak at them. Its glittering, beady eyes darted from Alice to one Tweedle and then to the other.

"JUB-JUB!" the bird screeched. It lunged forward and seized the Tweedles in its claws. Before Alice could react, the bird was in the air, flapping away.

The Tweedles were gone. The White Rabbit was gone. Everyone was gone.

Alice was quite alone.

CHAPTER SIX

On the shore of the Crimson Sea stood the castle of Iracebeth, the Red Queen. From the top of its tall, twisting spires flew her flag, a heart in flames fluttering as if it were truly on fire. The craggy walls were too steep to scale, and vultures wheeled over the sharp rocks below, testifying to the victims of the Queen's wrath who had been tossed off the battlements.

Surrounding the castle on one side were the barren red sands of Crims, and the fierce waters of the Crimson Sea battered the other. It was a fortress, and the dangerous aura around it matched the darkness at the heart of its ruler.

Inside, the Red Queen was screaming.

The frog footmen who lined the grand hall winced and gulped. Their pale legs trembled as they heard her footsteps stomping closer. The tall doors at one end of the hall suddenly banged open, revealing the Queen herself.

The first thing one noticed about the Red Queen was her positively gigantic head. That was also the second and third thing one noticed, and possibly all one might ever notice about her, as it really was extraordinarily huge. One might wonder why she never toppled over, as it looked extremely unbalanced to have a head so out of proportion. Her extremely large features protruded under a shock of bright red hair.

And right now—as it often was—her enormous face was contorted with anger.

"Someone has stolen three of my tarts!" she

roared. She seized the lapel of the nearest frog footman and leaned into his face. "Did you steal them?"

"No, Your Majesty," the frog stammered.

The Red Queen stalked down the long line of frogs, studying each of their faces through narrow eyes. At the end, she whirled on one particularly terrified frog.

"Did *you*?" she snarled.

"No, Your Majesty!" he cried.

Her black eyes gleamed with anger and triumph. One long finger reached out and wiped a telltale bit of jam from the side of the frog's mouth. His whole body shook as she held up her finger and sniffed the jam with her gigantic nose.

"Squimberry juice," she hissed.

"I was so hungry! I didn't mean to!" the frog wailed, nearly collapsing to the ground.

"OFF WITH HIS HEAD!" screamed the Red Queen.

Red Knights hurried into the hall and converged on the guilty frog.

"My family!" the frog pleaded. "Oh please, don't. No! I have little ones to look after!" His cries of despair faded as the Knights dragged him out the door.

The Queen turned to her Fish Butler, licking her lips with her hideous fat tongue. "Go to his house and collect the little ones. I love tadpoles on toast almost as much as I love caviar."

As she turned away, the Fish Butler suppressed a shudder of revulsion and anger. "Yes, Your Majesty."

"Drink!" the Red Queen barked. Almost immediately, the Fish Butler produced a drink with a straw and the Red Queen took a sip.

"Majesty?" said a new voice.

The Red Queen whirled, her face lighting up. Her whole manner became flirty and simpering as the man with the birthmark strode down the hall toward her. "Ilosovic Stayne," she purred. "You knave, where have you been lurking?"

The Knave of Hearts bowed low and took her extended hand. He kissed it, but barely, only brushing it briefly with his lips. The Red Queen sighed.

"Majesty, I found the Oraculum," he said, taking a step back. The Red Queen led the way into the throne room and watched him unroll the scroll on a table.

"That?" she said skeptically. "It looks so ordinary for an oracle."

"Look here," he said, his face serious. "On the Frabjous Day." He pointed to the illustration that had startled Alice earlier, of the blond knight battling the Jabberwocky.

The Queen squinted at it, and her face reddened with anger again. "I'd know that tangled mess of hair anywhere," she sneered. "Is it Alice?"

"I believe it is," said the Knave.

The Queen peered closer. She gnashed her teeth. "What is she doing with my darling Jabberwocky?"

The Knave cleared his throat and took a sideways step out of the Queen's reach. "She appears to be slaying it."

The Queen's eyes nearly popped out of her head. "She killed my Jabberbabywocky!" she shrieked.

"Not yet," the Knave said hurriedly. "But it will happen if we don't stop her."

"Find Alice, Stayne," said the Queen, her voice rising. "Find her!"

He gave another bow. "I will bring her head and lay it at your feet."

"No!" The Queen glared darkly at the scroll. "Bring the whole girl. I want to do it myself."

Stayne mounted his horse in the stableyard and looked coldly down at the bloodhound groveling on the paving stones. Bayard was a large, growling, brown dog with drooping ears and sad eyes, but it was said he had the sharpest nose in all the land. Three knights held him at bay with heavy ropes attached to the spiked collar around his neck. Bayard winced as the spikes pressed into his loose skin.

The Knave of Hearts had no pity in his gaze. "Find the scent of human girl and earn your freedom," he said to the dog.

"For my wife and pups as well?" asked Bayard, lifting his head. A spark of hope flared in his eyes.

"Everyone goes home," agreed the Knave.

The bloodhound lowered his nose to the ground and inhaled deeply. With a low growl, he bounded out through the castle gates with the Knights close behind him. Stayne leaned down to stroke his horse's neck.

"Hrrrrrrrmph," muttered the horse. "Dogs will believe anything."

* * *

Alice finally stopped running. She leaned against a tree, gasping for air. She had no idea where she was, but that had been true ever since she fell down the rabbit hole, so she was trying not to worry about it. She was surrounded by odd-looking trees, so it was some kind of wood, but a more normal one than the mushroom forest.

She pushed back her long golden hair and looked at the gashes on her arm. Blood welled up from the deep scratches and she flinched as she touched them. How could a dream-injury hurt so much?

"Ahem," said a voice above her. "It looks like you ran afoul of something with wicked claws."

"Yes, and I'm *still* dreaming!" Alice said indignantly. She looked up and realized she was talking to . . . part of a cat. The cat's disembodied head floated in the air above a nearby branch. Alice blinked at it, trying not to show her surprise.

"What did that to you?" asked the cat head.

Alice tried to remember the word Tweedledee had used. "Banner or Bander . . ."

"The Bandersnatch?" said the cat. His head disappeared suddenly, making Alice jump. And then, just as suddenly, the entire cat reappeared beside her on the ground. He sauntered closer to her with a seductive grin, all calm, casual sensuality. Something tugged at Alice's memory. She didn't know how she knew, but a name slipped into her mind: the Cheshire Cat. "I'd better have a look."

He inspected the wound for a moment. His pink tongue slid out and he reached to lick the gashes. Alice jerked away.

"What are you doing?" she asked.

He blinked slowly at her, looking amused. "It needs to be purified by someone with evaporating skills, or it will fester and putrefy."

That sounded quite horrible. But Alice didn't

want to be licked by a strange, giant cat whose various parts kept disappearing. "I rather you didn't. I'll be fine as soon as I wake up," she insisted.

"At least let me bind it for you," offered the Cheshire Cat, pulling out a white silk handkerchief. Alice let him tie the handkerchief firmly around her wound.

"What do you call yourself?" the cat asked as he worked.

"Alice."

He looked up sharply. "*The* Alice?"

"There's been some debate about that," Alice said.

The Cheshire Cat sidled away from her. "I never get involved in politics." He glanced around, as if making sure they were not being watched. "You'd best be on your way."

"Which way?" Alice asked. "All I want to do is wake up from this dream!"

The Cheshire Cat sighed heavily. "Fine. I'll take you to the Hare and the Hatter. But that's the end of it!" And with that, he vanished into thin air. Alice whirled around, then checked the branches again. There was no sign of the cat.

Finally he reappeared a short way away through the trees and gave her a curious look. "Coming?" he asked.

There was nothing she could do but follow him.

CHAPTER SEVEN

Even if Alice had not known that they were going to the home of the March Hare, she might have been able to guess who lived in the unusual house they found at the end of a tangled, hidden path. It was not an ordinary house. The roof was thatched with thick brown fur instead of straw or shingles. The long chimneys sticking out the top were shaped like rabbit ears. The doorknob was a soft white tuft of fur—unmistakably a rabbit's tail. Rabbit feet poked up out of the ground in place of a picket fence, and as Alice peered at the house she realized that it was peering right back at her with large pink rabbit eyes where its windows should be.

"Who? What? Where?" the Hare cried, wringing his paws and whipping around so his long ears flapped.

The March Hare was seated around a long table in his front yard, presiding over a tea party with only two other guests.

And from the looks of it, the party had been dragging on for a very long time. The white tablecloth was stained and threadbare, with glimpses of the pale wood underneath peeking through the holes. The chairs stood at lopsided angles, as if waiting for guests who would never come. None of the pieces of the tea set matched; in front of the Hare, a blue willowware cup stood alongside a cracked white saucer and a pale green teapot. The rest of the set was an odd mixture of cracked pots and chipped cups, many of them tipped over next to ancient brown tea stains no one had ever bothered to try cleaning up.

Slumped in one of the chairs was a pale, morose man wearing a ragged, scorched top hat. His threadbare dark velvet coat hung loosely on his thin frame, and his eyes were lined with circles of exhaustion. He was staring blankly into space as Alice and the Cheshire Cat approached.

Alice realized that the third member of the tea party was the Dormouse, who had somehow gotten around ahead of Alice again. The gruesome, bloody eye of the Bandersnatch hung like a trophy at her waist. She scowled when she saw Alice emerge from the trees.

But the man, who was called the Mad Hatter, had another reaction entirely. At the sight of Alice, he bolted upright. His whole being seemed to brighten; even his clothes perked up. Transfixed, he moved toward her, stepping directly up onto and over the table, as that was the shortest route to reach her. Alice shivered a little as he came closer, staring at her intently. There was something in his face that made her anxious for him. She knew she couldn't possibly deserve the delighted look he was giving her.

"It's you," said the Mad Hatter. He reached toward her golden hair, then pulled his hand back before touching her.

"No, it's not," the Dormouse snapped. "McTwisp brought us the wrong Alice."

The Mad Hatter shook his head. "It's absolutely Alice! You're absolutely Alice! I'd know you anywhere. I'd know him anywhere."

This time he did touch her, seizing her hand and pulling her back to the table. He stepped right up onto a chair and led her over the table the way he had come. Alice tried not to step on any teacups as they walked across the tablecloth. On the other side, the Hatter plunked her down in the chair next to his. She fidgeted nervously under his rapt gaze.

"Well, as you can see, we're still having tea,"

the Hatter explained. "It's all because I was obliged to kill Time waiting for your return. You're terribly late, you know . . . naughty. Well, anyway."

"Sugar?" asked the March Hare.

"Time became quite offended and stopped altogether," the Hatter continued. "Not a tick ever since."

"Raspberry jam—my favorite," the March Hare interjected.

"Time can be funny in dreams," said Alice.

The Hatter gave her an odd look. "Yes, yes, of course. But now you're back, you see" he hurried on, "and we need to get on to the Frabjous Day!"

He seized the Hare's left paw and the Dormouse seized his right. All three of them raised their clasped hands in the air. "Frabjous Day!"

"*Downal wyth Bluddy Behg Hid!*" they chanted in unison. Then they all dropped their hands and looked at her expectantly.

"What?" Alice said, confused.

The Cheshire Cat rolled his eyes. He was lounging against the rabbit's-foot fence, which occasionally twitched as if it found his presence rather irritating.

"Down with the Bloody Big Head," the cat translated for Alice. "Bloody Big Head being the Red Queen." He glanced around again, checking the trees with narrowed eyes.

"It's a secret language used by us," the Dormouse added. "The Underland Underground Resistance!" With a fierce expression, she raised her fist over her head.

The Cheshire Cat rolled his eyes again and wandered up to the table, sliding into one of the chairs in a graceful, feline way. He picked up a teapot with half its spout broken off and poured some tea into a delicate porcelain cup with faded butterflies painted on it.

"Come, come. We simply must commence with

the slaying and such," the Mad Hatter said, leaning forward emphatically. "Therefore, it's high time for Time to forgive and forget! Or forget and forgive, whichever comes first. Or is in any case most convenient. I'm waiting."

As he tugged on one of his ears, the March Hare had a terribly anxious expression. He peered at his pocket watch, tapped its face, and listened to it for a moment. Then, to Alice's surprise, the Hare dunked the watch into his teacup, pulled it out, and listened to it again. Tiny droplets of tea splattered onto the Hare's furry white chest.

He gasped. "It's ticking again!"

"Ooh!" The Hatter squealed.

The Cheshire Cat made a disgusted face and set his teacup down. "All this talk of blood and slaying has put me off my tea."

"Wonderful flavor," said the March Hare.

"The entire world is falling to ruin, and poor

Chessur's off his tea," the Mad Hatter said with thinly veiled hostility.

The Cat's tail lashed angrily. "What happened that day was not my fault!"

Suddenly enraged, the Hatter slammed both hands on the table. Cups and teapots went flying, and Alice just avoided getting hot tea spilled all over her skirt. She pushed her chair back from the table, alarmed by the Hatter's vehemence.

"You ran out on them to save your own skin!" the Hatter yelled at the Cat. "You *guddler's scuttish pilgar lickering*—" His speech disintegrated into wild, furious cursing, although it was all in a language Alice didn't know. "Shukem juggling slunking ur-pals. Bar lom muck egg brimni." But she didn't need to understand it to guess what he was expressing. His rage kept building, and the curses flew faster and faster, as if he couldn't stop himself. The Cheshire Cat slipped around the table and put his paws over Alice's ears.

"HATTER!" the Dormouse shouted.

The Mad Hatter jerked to a stop. He blinked, composing himself, and then sat down and picked up his teacup again. "Thank you," he said. "I'm fine."

This elicited a snort from the Cheshire Cat. "What's wrong with you, Tarrant?" he asked, letting go of Alice's ears and sitting in the chair on the other side of her. "You used to be the life of the party. You used to do the best *Futterwacken* in all of Witzend."

"Futter . . . ? What?" Alice echoed.

"*Futterwacken*," said the March Hare

"It's a dance," the Dormouse explained impatiently.

"On the Frabjous Day, when the White Queen once again wears the crown," said the Mad Hatter, lifting his chin. "On that day, I shall *Futterwacken* . . . vigorously." At that moment, the Hare's house bent over and tapped the Hare on the shoulder. "The Knave!" The March Hare gasped.

"Uh-oh!" cried the Cheshire Cat.

"Urg. The Knave!" the Dormouse added.

The March Hare shouted. "Hide her! Hide her!"

"Good-bye," said the Cheshire Cat, then he immediately vanished into thin air. The Hatter grabbed a small bottle off the table and shoved it into Alice's hands. It looked ominously familiar. "Drink this quickly," he commanded.

"Oh, no," Alice said, remembering the room with the locked doors and the little glass bottle she'd found there. She tried to resist, but the March Hare and the Mad Hatter forced the liquid down her throat. Before she could even shriek in protest, she was six inches tall.

And the indignity wasn't over. The Mad Hatter picked her up and dropped her in the nearest teapot, which luckily was empty of tea. Alice stumbled to her knees on the cold porcelain floor. Her hands scrabbled at the smooth walls curving up on either side of her. The Hatter peeked in the top, and she saw his enormous hand descending with the teapot lid.

"Mind your head," he said, and then the sky disappeared. Alice sat down huffily and crossed her arms. It was dim except for a stream of light from the spout. She could hear their voices outside quite clearly.

Soon Stayne arrived with his two Red Knights, following the bloodhound's nose. The bloodhound headed straight for the table and began sniffing furiously.

"Well," sneered the Knave of Hearts, "if it's not my favorite trio of lunatics."

"Would you like to join us?" asked the Dormouse.

"You're all late for tea!" shouted the March Hare, flinging a teapot at them (fortunately, not the one with Alice in it).

The Knave didn't bother to dodge. The teapot clattered harmlessly onto the path beside him as he surveyed the table with disdain. "We're looking for the girl called Alice."

Inside the teapot, Alice shuddered. She couldn't see Stayne, but she didn't like the sound of him. Why was everyone here so interested in her? And why wouldn't this dream simply end?

"Speaking of the Queen," said the Hatter as if the Knave had said something else, "here's a little song we used to sing in her honor."

All three of them burst into song at the same time, although their tunefulness left a bit to be desired. "Twinkle, twinkle, little bat!" they blared. "How I wonder where you're at!"

Alice buried her head in her hands. These were the people protecting her? What was she supposed to do if the Knave killed them or took them all prisoner? She'd be stuck in a teapot, six inches tall, and no one would ever think to look for her there. One day someone would buy the teapot from a stall in Portobello Road, and wouldn't they be surprised to find her dusty bones inside. Alice felt quite sorry for herself for a moment.

It's just a dream, she remembered. There's nothing to be scared of. It's just a dream.

Back outside, the song abruptly broke off as Stayne grabbed the Hatter around the neck. One Red Knight cracked the March Hare with his weapon, while the other seized a teapot (again, luckily not Alice's) and poured hot tea over the Dormouse's head. The Hare and the Dormouse yelped in pain.

"If you're hiding her, you'll lose your heads," growled the Knave.

"Already lost them," the Hatter said cheerfully, ignoring the thick hands around his neck. "All together now!"

The other two joined in for the rest of the song.

"Up above the world you fly, like a tea tray in the sky!" They all started laughing crazily. "Twinkle, twinkle, twinkle, twinkle!"

The Knave let go of the Hatter's neck and stalked around the table, looking disgusted.

Peering up the spout, Alice saw a large black nose appear. The bloodhound put his paws on the table, sniffing the teapot vigorously. The Hatter glanced at the Knave, who had turned his back for a moment. While the other two kept singing, the Hatter leaned down toward the bloodhound and took a chance.

"*Downal wyth Bluddy Behg Hid*," he whispered. He gave the teapot a significant look.

The bloodhound stopped dead. His large, sad eyes met the Hatter's haunted ones for a moment. Then the dog dropped to the ground and kept sniffing, pretending to catch a new trail. He hurried off into the woods again.

"Would you like some cream? Would you like

a slice of Battenberg? The March Hare said.

"Follow the bloodhound," snapped the Knave, ignoring him. He lingered suspiciously as the two Red Knights galloped after the hunting dog.

"Sugar? One lump or two?" the Dormouse offered.

"You're all mad," the Knave growled at the caterwauling partygoers.

"Pass the scones please?" the Dormouse replied.

The Mad Hatter lifted the lid of Alice's teapot. "Pardon," he said. "One moment."

He produced a pair of milliner's scissors from his pocket and quickly whipped up a miniature ensemble for Alice out of the tea cozy, a doily, and a swatch of her old dress. By now it was far too enormous for her to even drag around after her. The Hatter handed the new outfit down to Alice and closed the lid again to give her some privacy.

A few moments later, there was a tiny knock on the lid. He opened it and let her out. Wearing the remade outfit. Alice had to admit it fit much better and was a lot more comfortable than the dress her mother had insisted on that morning, corset or no corset.

"Ooh. I like it!" the Hatter cooed.

"Good thing the bloodhound is one of us, or you'd be . . ." the Dormouse said, as she drew her finger across her throat with an ominous noise.

The March Hare was wringing his paws again. "Best take her to the White Queen," he suggested. "She'll be safe there. Spoon . . ."

The Hatter swept his hat off and put it on the table beside her. "Your carriage, m'lady."

Alice raised her eyebrows. She looked from the Hatter to the hat and back again. "The hat?" she asked.

"Of course. Anyone can go by horse or rail," he said blithely. "But the best way to travel is by hat. Have I made a rhyme?"

Alice climbed up and sat on the hat, trying not to show how nervous this made her. The Dormouse trotted over and sat on the hat, too, shoving Alice aside. "Ooh! I love travelling by hat," she said. But the Hatter was shaking his head.

"Sorry, Mally," he said. "Just Alice, please."

The Dormouse huffed, annoyed, and climbed off again. She glared jealously at Alice as the Hatter swung the hat and Alice up onto his head.

"*Fairfarren*, all!" the Hatter sang, and started off into the woods.

"Whatcha mean?" wailed the March Hare behind them.

Alice and the Hatter ducked as a teapot hurtled past them. She couldn't help thinking the Knave was right about these three. They were all quite mad.

And yet . . . she had no one else. Mad or not, it seemed she was stuck with them.

CHAPTER EIGHT

Alice hung on tight as the Mad Hatter sauntered through the Tulgey Woods at a jaunty pace. Low branches brushed by right over her head and sunlight trickled through the green leaves. It was surprisingly peaceful, considering she'd nearly been eaten by a Bandersnatch and taken prisoner by a Knave not very long ago.

The Hatter was muttering something, but even the words she could make out sounded like nonsense:

Twas brillig, and the slithy toves
Did gyre and gimble in the wabe;
All mimsy were the borogroves,
And the mome raths outgrabe.

He warbled, like a child reciting a poem he'd memorized in school.

Alice carefully climbed down the hat and perched on his shoulder. "What was that?" she asked.

"What was what?" the Hatter asked. Then he continued:

The Jabberwock with eyes of flame.
The jaws that bite.
The claws that catch.

Beware of the Jabberwock, my son,
and the Frumious Bandersnatch.
He took his Vorpal Sword in hand.

The Vorpal Sword blade went snicker-snack
He left it dead, and with its head,
He went galumping back.

"It's all about you, you know?" he finished.

Alice thought it was high time she put this mad idea to rest. "I'm not slaying anything," she said firmly. "I don't slay. So put it out of your mind."

The Hatter stopped in his tracks. "Mmm . . . mind," he said, plucking her off his shoulder. He dropped her onto a log and kept walking. Astonished, Alice followed him. With her new tiny size, she had to run to keep up.

"Wait!" she called. "You can't leave me here!" At this size, she was reasonably afraid that a hawk might eat her. Or perhaps a very hungry squirrel. If they even had squirrels here . . . She hadn't seen any normal animals yet. The squirrels were probably ten feet tall and blue with dainty white gloves.

The Mad Hatter whirled around and stared at her. "You don't slay. . . . Do you have any idea what the Red Queen has done?" His voice became high-pitched, mimicking her. "You don't slay."

She spread her hands. It wasn't fair for him to mock her. "I couldn't if I wanted to," she protested. Where would a nice Victorian girl have learned how to slay things? She couldn't even kill the spiders and caterpillars that found their way into the house.

The Hatter put his hands on his hips. His gaze was accusing. "You're not the same as you were before," he said. "You were much more . . . muchier . . . you've lost your muchness," he finished, nodding as if that made perfect sense.

"My muchness?"

He crouched and poked her in the stomach with his finger. "In there," he said. "Something's missing."

The Hatter stood up and walked away again.

Alice frowned thoughtfully. What did he mean? How would he know if she was missing something? And . . . was she? After a moment, she ran after him.

"Tell me what the Red Queen has done," she called.

He stopped.

"It's not a pretty story."

"Tell me anyway," she insisted.

He scooped her up and plunked her back on his shoulder. They started forward again, although now Alice realized that the trees around them were changing. Instead of smooth brown trunks and fluttering green leaves, the foliage here was blackened and twisted, branches horribly charred like fingers clutching at the darkening sky.

The Hatter pushed through a thicket of branches, and they came out into a place where the earth was scorched and barren in a wide circle around them. He blinked, his eyes tearing up. His voice was hoarse with emotion as he began to tell the tale.

"It was here. I was Hatter to the Queen at the time. The Hightopp clan have always been employed at court."

His eyes stared blankly at the blackened place as he drifted back in his memory to the Horunvendush Day. His whole clan had been there—all the Hightopps, adults and children, festive in their shiny new top hats. He could remember them all cheering for the White Queen and her court as they rode in on gleaming white horses. Her long white robe flew out behind her as her horse trotted in the lead. Beside her rode the March Hare, the Cheshire Cat, and the White Rabbit, among others . . . all of them members of her court. And standing in the center of the clearing, holding the shining Vorpal Sword, was the White Knight, the one they had all come to see.

He remembered the sudden feeling of terror that brushed against all their hearts as enormous leathery wings blocked out the sun. The woods went dark around them. All the upturned faces were filled with awe and horror. They had never seen such a beast.

The White Knight—their hero, their champion, the one who was supposed to fight for them against all horrors—gaped at the terrifying creature, dropped the Vorpal Sword, and fled into the trees.

It took only a moment for panic to seep through the crowd. If the Knight was too afraid to fight, then there was no one to defend them all from the Jabberwocky. Screams broke out as everyone ran for his life, pushing and trampling anyone in the way. Fire streaming from the Jabberwocky's mouth blazed over their heads.

The Queen's horse reared, and the Queen lost her crown. The Hatter ran forward to grab the reins, losing his hat in the process. He led her to safety, but for one moment he looked back.

He saw one last thing before they escaped: the Knave of Hearts picked up the fallen sword and lifted it victoriously. With a howl, the Jabberwocky retreated, leaving carnage and disaster behind him . . . and only one surviving member of the once-sprawling Hightopp family.

The Hatter had returned to the scene later. His face was contorted with shock and horror as he crouched, touching the still-smoldering earth where his entire clan had died. Only one burned and trampled hat remained. The Hatter picked it up, brushed the soot off, and placed the wrecked hat firmly upon his head.

Alice watched him as he told his story. Her heart ached for him. Now she could understand his madness, and she couldn't help but pity him. She looked up at the scorched hat he still wore, then to his tormented face. He twitched, driven to the edge of his madness by guilt, helpless rage, and deep loss.

"Hatter?" Alice said. She remembered how the Dormouse handled these moments. "Hatter!" she shouted.

He jerked, pulling himself back from the abyss. "I'm fine," he said quickly.

"Are you?" Alice asked.

Instead of answering, the Hatter whipped his head around toward the dark trees that surrounded them. "Did you hear that?" he said softly. "I'm certain I heard something."

Alice strained her ears to hear what he had. "What?" she asked nervously.

He whipped around in the other direction. "Ooh. Red Knights!" he cried.

The bloodhound's chilling bay echoed through the woods. The Hatter slipped Alice into his waistcoat pocket and began to run. She clung to the brocade fabric with all her might as the world jolted and bumped around her. It was dusk now, and the lowering darkness made all the shadows seem extraterrifying.

The Hatter dodged trees and leaped over stumps, running flat out. He could see the edge of the woods ahead. But just before he reached it, a flash of red caught his eye from the right. He veered to run away, and a Red Knight stepped out in front of him. Quick as a wink, the Hatter spun in the other direction. But another Red Knight was there, waiting.

They were trapped.

CHAPTER NINE

"**G**o south to Trotter's Bottom," the Hatter hissed. It took Alice a moment to realize he was talking to her. "The White Queen's castle is just beyond."

She wanted to protest that she wouldn't leave him, but everything was moving too fast. The Hatter swept the hat off his head and bowed in a conciliatory way to the Red Knights. With his face hidden, he muttered, "Hold down tightly."

Perhaps if they didn't find her with him, they'd let him go. Alice did as she was told, leaping onto the hat. The Hatter immediately flung his arms into the air, sending the hat and Alice sailing over the treetops. She shut her eyes tight and clung to the brim of the hat as it flew out of the woods.

Behind her, she heard the Hatter yelling triumphantly. "DOWN WITH THE BLOODY RED QUEEN!" he bellowed. Her heart seized in her chest. She knew what he was doing—distracting the Red Knights. They would never let him go now, even if they had no evidence that he'd been helping her.

The hat landed lightly in the soft grass, far from the scene in the woods. Alice looked back at the forest, then south toward gently rolling hills. Dusk was vanishing into pitch darkness, and strange night sounds were starting to fill the air. Wherever she was going, it would be safer in the day, when she could see. She slipped under the hat and curled up on the grass to sleep.

It was not a very restful sleep, full of Bandersnatch teeth and dark wings and burning top hats and screaming children. Alice was almost relieved when she woke up to the sound of sniffing just outside the hat.

Then she realized who it must be. She sat up as the hat was flipped over and early morning light spilled over the grass around her. A giant wet nose came closer, sniffing her. It was the same bloodhound from the tea party, Bayard. He was alone.

Alice leaped to her feet, furious. "You turncoat!" she shouted, whapping his nose with her hand. "You were supposed to lead them away! The Hatter trusted you!"

Bayard jumped back a step, his long ears flapping. He looked down at her with his sad eyes and sagging face. "They have my wife and pups," he said mournfully.

This didn't make Alice any less angry. She thought of the Hatter's tormented expression as he stared across the blackened place. "What's your name?" she demanded.

"Bayard."

"Sit!" Alice said commandingly.

He cocked his head and looked at her curiously.

"Sit!" she said again, even more forcefully.

Bayard sat, amused if nothing else. Something seemed to occur to him. "Would your name be Alice by any chance?"

"Yes," said Alice, "but I'm not the one that everyone's talking about."

Bayard pawed at the dirt. "The Hatter would not have given himself up for just any Alice."

Alice couldn't handle the pang of guilt this caused her. Why had he done such a foolish thing? What if she wasn't the Alice he believed in so much? She couldn't be—there was no chance she was going to slay a monster anytime soon.

"Where did they take him?" she asked. It was easier to change the subject than to argue about her Alice-ness.

"To the Red Queen's castle at Salazen Grum," said the dog.

The soft grass rippled around Alice as she turned to look at the Hatter's worn old hat, remembering the pain in his eyes. She turned back to the bloodhound, resolute.

"We're going to rescue him."

The bloodhound shook his head. "That is not foretold."

"I don't care!" said Alice. "He wouldn't be there if it weren't for me."

Bayard stood up, his fur standing on end as he shivered anxiously. "The Frabjous Day is almost upon us. You must prepare to meet the Jabberwocky."

"From the moment I fell down that rabbit hole, I've been told what I must do and who I must be. I've been shrunk, stretched, scratched, and stuffed into a teapot. I've been accused of being Alice and of not being Alice. But this is my dream! I'll decide where it goes from here."

Bayard's claws dug into the ground. "If you diverge from the path—"

"I make the path!" Alice shouted.

She was so commanding, the bloodhound lay down at her tiny feet. Alice grabbed his long ear and climbed up to sit on his shoulders. The wrinkles of skin and short brown fur around his neck prickled against her bare hands.

"Take me to Salazen Grum," she ordered. "And don't forget the hat."

Bayard obediently picked up the hat in his teeth and ran. Alice held onto his black spiked collar. He ran and ran and ran, speeding across strange landscapes like nothing Alice had ever seen before. At one point, his paws sank into a swamp of viscous red mud. He held the hat high to keep it clean as he waded through. The mud stuck to his fur and his paws in gooey clumps that gradually dried and flaked off as he kept running.

They reached a wide red desert, but not so wide that Alice couldn't see the dark castle rising on the far side. Red sand whipped her face as Bayard's paws pounded across the flat surface. She crouched lower, feeling the sun beat down on her back. A roaring reached her ears as they drew closer, and she realized there was an ocean on the far side of the castle. Waves pounded tempestuously against the shore below tall black cliffs.

The walls of the castle seemed to get higher and steeper and more foreboding as they ran toward it. Bayard slowed down as they approached the moat, a stinking circle of water with no bridge across it at the moment. Large, round, lumpish objects floated in the water, pale and bloated. Alice stared at them for a second, then realized they were the heads of the executed. She closed her eyes and shuddered.

"There's only one way across," the bloodhound said, pausing on the edge of the moat. He looked sadly down at the clutter of floating heads.

Alice followed his gaze to the grim moat, then took a deep breath for courage.

"Lost my muchness, have I?" she muttered. She swung down from Bayard's shoulder and steeled herself. She crouched and leaped onto the first head, landing with an unsettlingly squishy thud. Quickly she jumped to the next head, then the next, and as fast as she could, she made it across the moat, leaping from head to head. They bobbed and smushed sickeningly under her feet and she was horribly certain she'd stepped on someone's eye as she ran.

Finally she stumbled onto the grass on the far side and fell to her knees. This nightmare was far worse than the one she usually had.

At length she pushed herself upright and stared up at the impossibly high wall. It would be hard enough for a normal-size girl to climb it, let alone one who was only six inches tall.

Then again . . .

Alice looked down at the base of the wall. After a moment of searching, she found what she wanted—a crack just big enough for a six-inch girl to squeeze through. She turned and called back to the bloodhound.

"Bayard! The hat!"

Bayard picked up the hat in his teeth. Turning in circles like a discus thrower, he released the hat, and it and the hat sailed high across the moat and over the wall.

Alice wriggled through the crack in the wall. For a moment she was afraid she'd get stuck—yet another unpleasant way to die—but at last she tumbled out on the other side and found herself in a garden. It was neater and better-tended than the first garden she'd been in, and the flowers looked less likely to criticize her, given that they had no faces or opinions at all.

Alice crouched in the bushes and peered out onto a great lawn, wide and green and smooth. It reminded her a little of Lady Ascot's great lawn, in fact . . . not least because there were people playing croquet on it.

But these were not ordinary people. Alice could guess right away which one was the Red Queen. A tiny crown sat atop her gigantic head, and her face was red with glee as she whacked away with her mallet. The three courtiers she played with were no less peculiar looking. One of the women had the largest nose Alice had ever seen, while the other had ears that hung down nearly to her waist. The third was a man with a huge protruding belly, so large that Alice couldn't believe he could even see over it to hit the ball.

WHACK!

A small cry of pain followed the loud thwacking

sound. The three courtiers cheered and applauded. The Queen sniffed and moved forward, swinging her mallet again. Once more Alice heard a tiny cry of pain after the mallet hit. She glanced around for the source, but it wasn't until the ball rolled closer to her that she realized what was happening.

The ball wasn't a ball at all. It was a tiny hedgehog with its four feet tied together. Its spikes were matted and filthy, and it rolled to a stop with its face buried in the grass. Alice could hear it panting and gasping for air. It was the saddest little creature she'd ever seen.

THWACK! The Queen hit the hedgehog again, and now Alice realized that the mallet was not an ordinary mallet either. Instead, it was a miserable flamingo with its legs bound together and clutched in the Queen's hands. Each time its beak hit the hedgehog, both creatures flinched in agony.

The last *thwack* sent the hedgehog ball rolling right into the bushes at Alice's feet. She crouched immediately and started to untie it. The hedgehog yelped with fear.

"Splendid shot!" shouted one of the Queen's guards.

"Shh," Alice said to the Hedgehog. "I want to help you." Her hands shook with anger as she worked the tight knots. What kind of monster could do this to an innocent animal?

"Where's my ball!" the Red Queen bellowed. "PAGE!"

The last rope slipped free, and the hedgehog stumbled to its paws. It gave Alice a mute, bewildered look for a moment, then staggered away into the foliage. Alice was about to follow it when a pair of furry white feet suddenly appeared in front of her.

She looked up and up and up into the face of the White Rabbit. To her surprise, he was now dressed as a court page. Did he work for the Red

Queen? But then why would he have brought Alice to this world?

"Well!" he said, apparently as surprised as she was. "If it isn't the wrong Alice. What brings you here?"

"I've come to rescue the Hatter," said Alice.

The White Rabbit practically laughed in her face. "You're not rescuing anyone, being the size of a gerbil."

That was probably true. Alice thought for a moment. "Well, do you have any of that cake that made me grow before?"

"*Upelkuchen*?" said the Rabbit. He patted his pockets. "Actually, I might have some left." His paws dug through his clothes until he unearthed a piece of cake. Alice seized it and shoved it in her mouth.

"Not all of it!" cried the White Rabbit, but it was too late. Alice shot upward. Buttons flew off her torn garments; the makeshift outfit the Hatter had given her split right down the seams instantly.

"Oh, no, stop!" the Rabbit cried, wringing his paws. "No, no, don't—don't do that!"

"PAGE!" the Red Queen screamed.

"Oh, dear," said the White Rabbit.

Alice burst right through the shreds of her clothes and popped out of the bushes.

Alice looked down at the Red Queen and her courtiers, who were gaping at this strange naked girl who had suddenly grown out of the foliage. Luckily the tall bushes hid all but her head and shoulders, but Alice still felt quite embarrassed. She wished she was wearing anything, even a corset, right now. Poor Mother would have died of shock.

The Red Queen's eyebrows came down into a menacing scowl. Everyone's gaze went from Alice to the Queen as she pointed a long, shaking finger at Alice's towering head.

"And WHAT is *this*?"

CHAPTER TEN

"I t's a 'who,' Majesty!" cried the White
Rabbit, popping out of the bushes behind
Alice. "This is . . . um . . ."

"Um?" echoed the Red Queen.

"From Umbradge," Alice added hastily.

The Queen looked skeptical. "What happened to
your clothes?"

"I outgrew them," said Alice, quite honestly.
Sensing this would not be enough of an answer, she
began to improvise. "I've been growing an awful
lot lately. I tower over everyone in Umbradge. . . .
They laugh at me. So I've come to you, hoping

you might understand what it's like."

There was a long, tense pause as the Red Queen studied her with narrowed eyes. At last she said, "My dear girl. Anyone with a head that large is welcome in my court."

"Ha-ha-ha-ha-ha-ha-ha-ha!" chorused the courtiers, doubling over with peals of exaggerated laughter.

"SOMEONE FIND HER SOME CLOTHES!" bellowed the queen. "USE THE CURTAINS IF YOU MUST, BUT CLOTHE THIS ENORMOUS GIRL!" A flurry of activity ensued as pages and servants went dashing off in all directions. The Queen gave Alice a conspiratorial look. "You'll be my new favorite."

The courtiers weren't laughing anymore. They huffed jealously and glared at Alice in a threatening, competitive way. Lady Long Ears looked especially displeased.

But Alice didn't have even a moment to think

about that, as she was whirled off to the castle and draped with enough fabric to cover Buckingham Palace. Long red velvet curtains tied with a gold-colored rope restored her decency, but the whole ensemble looked rather strange. She tugged a loose edge over her shoulder as she hurried down a long hall after the Red Queen.

All around her, animals were hard at work doing things they were never intended to do. She could see that hedgehogs and flamingos were not the only ones suffering in the Red Queen's court. Overhead, exhausted birds flapped their wings painfully, trying to stay aloft to hold up the Queen's lamps in their beaks. At the edges of the hall, the tables and chairs had no legs; instead, they were held up by monkeys, their furry arms trembling with exertion. The footfrogs that stood at attention as the Queen swept past all looked petrified.

They reached the Queen's elaborate throne

room, which was furnished in much the same way. An ornate throne stood at the far end on legs made of terrified spider monkeys. Without so much as a glance at the monkeys, the Queen plopped down on the throne, and they all strained under her weight. The Red Queen kicked off her shoes and waved one small hand in the air.

"I need a pig here!" she called.

Immediately, a small pig hurried over from an alcove and lay down belly-up in front of her. The Queen put her bare feet on its belly and sighed contentedly.

"I love a warm pig belly for my aching feet," she said. She turned her attention to Alice. "Would you like one, Um?"

"No, thank you," Alice replied.

"Sit! Sit!" the Red Queen told Alice.

Alice gingerly sat on the largest chair she could find, doing her best to keep her newly enormous weight off the poor monkeys underneath her. She could see their long drooping tails spiraling out on either side of the chair.

The Red Queen flapped her hands at the three courtiers. "Go away," she ordered. They left, casting dark jealous looks at Alice. "Where are my Fatboys?" the queen went on. "You must meet them! Fatboys!"

To Alice's horror, the pair that were dragged into the room were Tweedledum and Tweedledee. Their cheerful round faces were glum now, and garishly painted. White powder had been heavily applied and red hearts had been painted on their cheeks. Red-heart lips added to the monstrous look, and a long gold belt bound them together around their waists. Their eyes were lowered to the marble floor, their whole posture downtrodden and hopeless.

"There they are!" squealed the Red Queen, clapping her hands. "Aren't they adorable? And they have the oddest way of speaking. Speak, boys! Amuse us!

"Speak!"

Tweedledee lifted his eyes and saw Alice for the first time. He nudged his brother with his elbow. "Is that being . . . ?" he started.

Alice lifted one finger to her lips and shook her head slightly.

"No, it isn't," said Tweedledum, a spark of hope flaring in his eyes. "Not a bit. No."

Tweedledee blinked, puzzled. He had missed Alice's gesture. "Contrariwise, I believe it is so—"

"No!" Tweedledun cut him off. "It ain't so. No-how!" He stomped on his brother's foot to silence him. Disgruntled, Tweedledee pinched him, and Tweedledum pinched back.

The Queen laughed raucously. "I love my Fat-boys. Now, get out."

Casting last, pleading glances at Alice, the

Chapter Ten

Tweedles rolled out of the room. As they exited, they passed Stayne, the Knave of Hearts, coming in. The Red Queen clasped her hands and fluttered her eyelashes at him seductively. Stayne repressed a shudder, but when the Queen extended her hand to him, he kissed it.

A pair of Red Knights left the room. Stayne noticed Alice and his eyebrows went up. "And who is this lovely creature?" He took Alice's hand, looking at her intensely. Alice tried to look blandly polite and uninteresting, as her mother had often tried to teach her for meeting crowds of people at horrible garden parties. But her heart beat a little faster with fear at being so close to the man who'd been hunting her. She did not like the way he studied her.

"Um, my new favorite," said the Queen, answering Stayne's question.

"Does she have a name?" asked the Knave.

"Um," said the Queen.

The Knave of Hearts turned to Alice with an oily smile. "I believe your name has slipped the Queen's mind."

The Red Queen leaned forward and smacked him hard. "Her name is *Um*. Idiot."

"Any luck with the prisoner?" the Queen asked.

Alice's ears perked up. Prisoner?

"He's stubborn," grumbled the Knave. His birthmark flared brightly across his face.

"You're too soft," snapped the Queen. "Bring him!"

He did not talk back to the Queen, but Alice could see a dangerous anger smoldering in his eyes.

A clatter at the door announced the arrival of the guards with their prisoner. Alice had to stifle a gasp as they dragged the Hatter into the room, chained by his hands and feet. Bruises covered his face and blood soaked through his clothes. He'd clearly been roughed up. His eyes had an empty, faraway stare. The Queen seized a hunk of his hair and lifted his head to meet her eyes, but he barely seemed to see her.

"We know Alice has returned to Underland," snarled the Queen. "Do you know where she is?"

The Hatter didn't respond. Scowling, the Queen clapped her hands in front of his face, and he jerked back to the moment. His eyes cleared and focused a bit, but he still didn't see Alice.

"I've been considering things that begin with the letter *M*: moron, mutiny, murder, malice . . ." he said.

"We're looking for an *A* word now," the Queen responded. "Where is Alice?"

The Hatter furrowed his brow as if he were thinking hard. After a moment, a look of inspiration crossed his face, then paused and retreated. He considered again for a long while and finally shrugged.

"Who? That wee little boy? I wouldn't know."

The Red Queen scowled even more. "What if I take off your head, will you know then?"

The Hatter snickered.

"Stop that!" the Queen snapped.

Suddenly the Hatter's gaze found Alice. Surprised at her new size, he gave her a wry smile, then turned back to the Queen, smarmy and unctuous.

"What a regrettably large head you have," he said smoothly. "I should very much like to hat it."

"Hat it?" echoed the Queen.

"Yes. I used to hat the White Queen, you know," he said. "But there wasn't very much for me to work with, poor dear. Her head is so small."

"It's tiny! A pimple of a head!" The Red Queen snorted.

"But this!" the Hatter went on, acting rapturous. "What I could do with this monument . . . this orb. Nay, this magnificently heroic globe!"

"What could you do?" asked the Queen, intrigued despite herself.

The Hatter lifted his bound hands in a helpless gesture.

"Untie him, Stayne!" the Queen ordered. "How can he work if his hands are bound?"

The Knave rolled his eyes, but he unbound the Hatter's hands without arguing. The Hatter began to circle the Queen, his hands outlining elegant images in the air.

"Well, then, shall it be a bonnet or a boater," he mused, "or something for the boudoir?" His voice rose in pitch, becoming more manic as he went on. "Cloche, dunce hat, death cap, coif, snood, barboosh, pugree, yarmulke, cockle-hat, porkpie, tam-o'-shanter, billycock, bicorn, tricorn, bandeau, bongrace, fan-tail, nightcap, garibaldi, fez . . ."

Alice could see he would lose the Queen if he wasn't pulled back from the edge of madness again.

She pretended to sneeze into her hand so she could let out a muffled: "HATTER!"

He jerked back, present again. "Fez . . . Fez."

The Red Queen looked down her nose at Alice and Stayne. "Leave us."

Alice was only too glad to get up and leave that room, although she worried about leaving the Hatter alone with the Queen. On the other hand, at least it took the Knave away from him; he was obviously more suspicious of the Hatter than the Red Queen was.

CHAPTER ELEVEN

A cross the desert and hills, far on the other side of Underland, Bayard the bloodhound galloped across the bluffs toward the White Queen's castle.

In her courtyard, Mirana, the White Queen, was speaking with a Loyalist.

"The trees seem sad. Have you been speaking with them?"

"Yes, Your Majesty," the loyalist answered.

"Perhaps a bit more kindly. Would you all excuse me for a moment? Thank you."

Bayard staggered into the Queen's courtyard and

she crouched beside him, stroking his long brown ears and holding out a dish of water for him as he panted.

"What news, Bayard?" she asked in her soft, kind voice.

"Alice has returned to Underland." He gasped.

A smile lit up the Queen's lovely face. "Where is she now?"

"In Salazen Grum," he admitted, flinching with guilt. "Forgive me, I allowed her to divert from her destined path."

The Queen shook her head, her smile widening. "No, no, no, no. That is exactly where she will find the Vorpal Sword," she explained. "We have our champion! Rest now. You've done well."

Exhausted, the bloodhound collapsed to the ground.

In the garden of the Red Queen's castle, Alice

searched through the bushes. She passed the hedgehog, curled under a wide leaf and cleaning the caked dirt off his fur.

"Have you seen a hat around here?" she asked him.

The hedgehog pointed and watched as Alice spotted the Hatter's hat, made a delighted noise, and picked it up. With loving care, she wiped off the mud and straightened it out. Whatever it took to save the Hatter, she'd have his hat waiting for him at the end.

Evening had fallen, and inside the Red Queen's bedchamber, the Queen stood at the window with her Knave behind her.

"You must find Alice, Stayne," said the Queen, her nails digging into the wood of the window frame. "Without the Jabberwocky, my sister's followers will surely rise against me." A note of bitterness crept into her voice. "Ugly little sister . . . why do they adore her and not me?"

"I cannot fathom it," answered the Knave of Hearts, careful not to touch her. "You are far superior in all ways."

"I know," said the Queen without a hint of sarcasm. "But Mirana can make anyone fall in love with her: men, women, even the furniture." She glanced dismissively at the captive animals that held up tables and chairs and lamps around the room. She didn't even see them as animals anymore; to her they were simply furniture, and to discover they had any feelings might astonish or amuse her.

"Even the King," said the Knave of Hearts quietly.

The Red Queen turned her dark gaze to the window again, letting it travel slowly down to the grim moat of bobbing heads below. "I had to do it. He would have left me."

"Majesty," the Knave said, "isn't it better to be feared than loved?"

"Not certain anymore," she answered. Some internal struggle seemed to take place, and finally she burst out: "Oh, let her have the rabble! I don't need them. I have you." She leaned her enormous head back, looking at him with big, dewy eyes. "I do have you, don't I, Stayne?"

He managed a smile, which, fortunately for him, seemed to be enough of a reply for the Queen.

Alice ducked as she entered the Queen's dressing room. Strange stars twinkled outside the window in a velvety night sky. The room had only one occupant: the Hatter, surrounded by ribbons, bows, veils, and feathers. He hummed happily as he worked. Already several huge, colorful hats were perched on dummies and scattered across the floor.

"They're wonderful!" Alice cried with sincere

awe. "You must let me try one on."

Instantly the Hatter swept a splendid hat off a shelf and perched it on her head. Tall blue feathers bobbed down in her face and tiny diamonds sparkled around the wide rim. Fake little bluebirds nested among the feathers and an enormous silver veil cascaded down her back. Alice giggled as she whirled around. If only the hats her mother attempted to make her wear were this much fun!

She struck a "grand lady" pose, imagining Lady Ascot. Then she grabbed another hat and perched it on the Hatter's head. He immediately struck the same pose, and they both laughed.

"It's good to be working at my trade again," said the Hatter, removing his hat and stroking it lovingly.

Alice took off her hat as well. She gently placed it back on the shelf. "It's just a pity you had to make them for *her*."

Chapter Eleven

The Hatter looked around the room as if he'd just realized what he'd done. His face filled with remorse and self-recrimination, and he slumped mournfully.

"What is the hatter with me? Hatter... Mmmmm, ma." he asked.

Suddenly, fury seized him. He swiped his hand across the table, sending all the tools of his trade flying.

Alice jumped in front of him, knocked the scissors away, and took his face in her hands, forcing him to look at her. "Hatter!"

He froze, and she could see the fear in his eyes. "Have you any idea why a raven is like a writing desk? I don't like it here, it's terribly crowded. Have I gone mad?" he whispered.

She felt his forehead with her hand as her father had done to her so many years ago. "I'm afraid so," she said. "You're entirely bonkers. But I'll tell you a secret . . . all the best people are."

The Hatter straightened his shoulders with pride. Even his clothes seemed to puff up.

Alice reached behind a box and produced the Hatter's own bedraggled top hat. His eyes filled with emotion as Alice put it on his head and tapped the rim proudly. "That's better," she said. "You look yourself again."

The Hatter was too overwhelmed to speak. He took off the hat and pressed it to his heart with an expression full of gratitude.

They were suddenly interrupted by the piercing sound of the Red Queen's voice. "Hat man!" she shrieked from the next room. "Where are my hats? I am not a patient monarch!"

The Hatter seemed to come to. He seized Alice's hand intensely, keeping his voice low. "I'm told she keeps the Vorpal Sword hidden in the castle. Find it, Alice. Take it to the White Queen.

Alice glanced down at the long, thick chain binding his ankle to the wall. She still wasn't sure about slaying any Jabberwocky, but she *could* think of something else she'd like to do with that sword.

"We'll go to the White Queen together," she said, taking his other hand. They looked into each other's eyes for a long moment, and Alice found herself wishing she weren't quite so absurdly huge.

The Hatter grinned ruefully, evidently having the same thought. "Why is it you're always too small or too tall?" he asked.

Alice slipped away to find her courtroom while the Red Queen was busy trying on hats. The Tweedles were stationed outside the door, one on each side.

"Tweedles!" Alice said happily when she spotted them. Considering how silly and maddening they could be, she was surprised at how delighted she was to see them. She only wished it were in better, less *prisoneresque* circumstances.

They each took one of her hands and shook them vigorously. "Alice!" they cried in unison.

"Howdoyedo again," said Tweedledum.

"Where's the Rabbit—" Alice started, but Tweedledee interrupted.

"How is it you're being so great big?" he asked.

"She ain't great big," said his brother. "This is how she normal is."

"I'm certain she is smaller when we met," insisted Tweedledee.

"She had drank the *pishsalver*, to get through the door. Recall it?" said Tweedledum.

"Where's the Rabbit?" Alice asked again.

"Over theres!" they chorused together, but each pointed in the opposite direction. Alice sighed.

These two weren't exactly the most reliable guides, but when they set off, she had little choice but to follow them.

Much to her surprise, after some walking and climbing stairs and roundabout wandering, they actually came to the White Rabbit. He was whispering with a chambermaid, but as they got closer, Alice realized the maid was actually the Dormouse in disguise.

"What are you doing here?" the Dormouse asked.

"I'm rescuing the Hatter," Alice replied.

"*I'm* rescuing the Hatter," the Dormouse corrected her.

"He told me that the Vorpal Sword is hidden in the castle. Help me find it," Alice said.

The Tweedles immediately hurried off, but the Dormouse and White Rabbit remained. "I don't take orders from big, clumsy, galumphing—" The Dormouse stood her ground.

Alice loomed over her and pointed imperiously. "Shoo!"

With a humiliated squeak, the Dormouse stalked off. Alice turned and saw that the White Rabbit was still there.

"What is it, McTwisp?" she asked.

He paused, then looked up at her with serious eyes.

"I know where the sword is."

Chapter Twelve

The White Rabbit drew himself up, looking ruffled, and led her down the hall without another word. Alice followed him through winding passages and down cold stone staircases lined with musty tapestries. Finally, he pushed open a creaking wooden door and led her out into a wide courtyard. He stopped outside the stables and pointed with one trembling white paw.

"The sword's hidden inside. Be careful, Alice," he said.

Alice bent down to push the door open. A horrible stench hit her nostrils, and both she and the

White Rabbit covered their faces, trying not to gag.

"I know that smell," Alice said in a muffled voice suffused with horror.

Sure enough, when she'd worked up the courage to look inside, she spotted the Bandersnatch lying in its stall with its huge ugly bulldog head on its paws. It moaned, clawing at the blood-soaked straw underneath it. Even in the dim light, Alice could see the empty socket oozing blood and goop where the eye had been.

"I'm not going in there!" Alice cried. "Look what that thing did to my arm!" She held out her scratched arm and noticed that the wound had gotten much worse. It was larger and very swollen, with angry red welts rising around the scratches.

The White Rabbit gasped and clapped his paws to his face in horror. "Dear, oh, dear!" he fretted. "Why haven't you mentioned this?"

Alice studied her arm, tilting it back and forth

in the moonlight. "It wasn't this bad before," she pointed out.

The Rabbit's breath was coming in fast pants. He flapped his paws as if trying to revive himself, but in the end he failed and fell over in a dead faint.

Well, that's useful, Alice thought wryly, looking down at the collapsed rabbit. She looked back at the castle, considering her next move.

It took some searching, but eventually she found Mallymkun. The Dormouse was standing in an upstairs hall, looking into a room; then she shut the door. "Hatter, where are you? Hatter?" she called out in a whisper.

"Mallymkun!" Alice called, hurrying up. "Do you still have the Bandersnatch eye?"

"Right here," said the Dormouse, hitching up her maid's skirt to reveal that she was wearing her breeches underneath. The Bandersnatch eye still hung at her waist.

"I need it," Alice said.

"Come and get it!" Mallymkun replied.

Alice quickly and easily grabbed the eye from the Dormouse.

"Hey! Give it back," the Dormouse said, drawing her hatpin sword and brandishing it dangerously.

But Alice missed the Dormouse's threat; she was running pell-mell down the long staircases, hoping she remembered the right way to the stables.

Alice sensed someone behind her, practically breathing down her neck. She tried to move away, but he grabbed the arm that had been scratched by the Bandersnatch. Alice let out a yelp of pain. Ignoring her cry, the man pushed her against the wall. It was Stayne, the Knave.

"I like you, Um," he murmured. "I like largeness."

He leaned in for a kiss as Lady Long Ears went past.

"Get away from me!" Alice cried, kicking Stayne

as hard as she could. She didn't look back as she ran away, but she could feel the heat of his glare all the way down the hall.

Finally, Alice found a familiar-looking door and stumbled out into the paved courtyard. The White Rabbit still lay prone on the cobblestones. Alice hurried past him and held her breath as she entered the stable.

The Bandersnatch saw her coming and growled fiercely. Even wounded, it was terrifying. Its shark-like teeth gnashed as if it were daring her to come closer and get eaten.

"I have your eye," said Alice, holding it aloft.

The monster's demeanor changed instantly. Its tail lashed along the floor and it whined, leaning toward the eye with a piteous expression. Alice slowly lifted the bar of the stall door and eased inside. She held out the eye and he whined again, scrabbling toward it across the straw. Alice carefully put it near him on the floor, and he started sniffing it frantically. With another whine, he pulled the eye closer with his paws to examine it more closely.

While he was distracted, Alice squeezed past him to the back of the stall, where she found a low rectangular object covered by a tarp. When she pulled the tarp back, it revealed an ornate metal chest—exactly the sort of thing one might keep a Vorpal Sword in.

Unfortunately, it was secured with a large lock . . . exactly what one might use to keep Vorpal Sword–stealers *out*. Sweating and shivering, poisoned by her wound, she tugged at the lock.

Disheartened and feverish, Alice slumped to the ground. She'd been running on adrenaline, but the pain in her arm was starting to catch up with her. She felt feverish and woozy. She could barely muster the strength to pull back her sleeve and look at the swollen, infected wound again. Carefully, she tried touching it, but pulled back quickly with a stifled cry of pain.

The Bandersnatch was still busy fussing over his eye, but that couldn't last all night. Sweating and shivering, Alice pulled at the lock, then halfheartedly kicked it with frustration. Her vision was starting to dim. She blinked, shaking her head.

And the world went black.

CHAPTER THIRTEEN

The sun was peering over the distant hills, lighting flurries of dust from the red desert below. Inside the castle, the Red Queen stood in front of one of her mirrors, wearing one of the Hatter's enormous red hats. The Hatter tilted his head, regarding her with aloof disdain.

"No," the Queen said, removing the hat.

The Queen's courtiers gasped with forced delight and began to flutter around her.

"You are stunning in that hat!" cried the man with the enormous belly.

"Yes. Next," the Queen said.

The Hatter took off the Queen's hat and replaced it with another—this one featuring a huge brim that hid half her face. The Hatter smiled with satisfaction.

"Your Majesty has never looked better," cooed the woman with the gigantic nose. "Another," the Queen said. But before the Hatter could hat her head again, Lady Large Nose's nose fell to the floor.

"You dropped something," the Hatter said.

The woman's eyes widened as she realized what had happened. She felt for her nose, but found only her actual nose, which was quite a normal size. With a gasp, she grabbed the fake and quickly turned away to reattach it.

The Hatter's eyes narrowed suspiciously. Now he spotted the straps above the man's pants which held his false protruding belly in place. The woman turned back around with her long nose reattached, and the Hatter laughed out loud, not a mad laugh this time, but one of genuine amusement. The courtiers gave him a nervous look.

"Oh. Never mind him," the Queen said from under her hat, having missed the whole exchange. "He's mad." She waved one hand dismissively. "Come along."

The female courtier with the long ears came rushing into the room. She hurried over and whispered into the Queen's ear. The Queen's face became redder and redder as she listened. Finally she bellowed, "STAYNE!" and everyone within hearing distance was quite happy he was not the Knave of Hearts.

Meanwhile, down in the stables, Alice was just waking up to find the ominous visage of the Bandersnatch looming over her. Somehow he'd managed to shove his eye back into its socket, where it now stared upward uselessly. And yet this seemed to please the creature—so much so that he hadn't eaten Alice in her sleep.

Alice noticed a large key on a chain hanging around the Bandersnatch's neck. It must be the key to the chest! Keeping her eyes on the Bandersnatch, she reached for it, then froze as the monster lowered his head to sniff her arm and the wound he'd inflicted. A sharp bolt of pain ran up to her shoulder, but she refused to be deterred. Reaching forward again, she pulled the key off his neck.

But before she could turn to the chest, the Bandersnatch's long, thin tongue coiled out of its mouth. He began to gently lick her wound, and to her surprise, his tongue was soothing and cool. With a sigh, she let him lick the wound clean. When he stopped, the infection was miraculously gone and the swelling had gone down. Alice moved her arm around, realizing the pain was gone, too.

Chapter Thirteen

The Bandersnatch tilted his head at her, one eye askew.

"I suppose this makes us even now," said Alice, but she had to admit to herself that she now felt quite a bit more warmed to the horrible, toothy creature.

The key slid perfectly into the lock on the chest, and when Alice lifted the lid, she found a gleaming sword inside. She knew instantly that it was the Vorpal Sword—no other sword could be so beautiful. It was made of shiny silver with an ornate handle. Alice lifted it up to the light and saw runes engraved on the blade.

The Bandersnatch shuffled aside to let her leave the stall, and Alice found herself patting him on the nose as she went by. She carried the sword out into the courtyard, unaware of the peril that was waiting for her back inside the castle. . . .

* * *

"Um forced herself on me!" the Knave lied, talking fast. He knelt before the Queen in the great hall, surrounded by curious courtiers and footfrogs who were rather enjoying the spectacle of the great Knave of Hearts in trouble for once.

"I told her my heart belongs to you," Stayne wheedled, taking the Queen's hand. "But she's obsessed with me!"

The Queen turned bright red with rage. "Off with her head!" she screamed.

In the Queen's dressing room, the Dormouse was trying to pick the lock of the chain around the Hatter's ankles. Her hatpin kept bending in the sturdy lock, and she made a small noise of irritation.

"Stand back, Mallymkun!" said a voice from the door.

The Dormouse and the Hatter both looked

up at once. Standing in the doorway was Alice, victoriously wielding the Vorpal Sword high over her head. She gave the Hatter a triumphant look.

"How's this for *muchness*?" Alice asked. She swung the sword toward his chain.

"No! No!" cried the Hatter, wrenching the chain out of her way. Alice staggered forward and blinked at him in surprise. He hurried on, trying to explain. "It mustn't be used for anything but—"

"Arrest that girl for unlawful seduction!" cried another voice. The Knave of Hearts stood in the doorway, pointing at Alice. His Red Knights clattered in behind him and headed straight for her.

"Hatter!" called the Dormouse. Alice raised the sword to fight, but—

"Take it to the White Queen!" the Hatter cried.

"I'm not leaving without you!" Alice objected.

"Go!" he called out.

But Alice was hesitant. The Hatter grabbed two bolts of fabric and threw them, knocking the Red Knights down. The Knave then unsheathed his sword. The Hatter picked up a mannequin and used it to block Stayne's blows. Stayne hovered over him, driving him back against the table. The Hatter reached over his shoulder and grabbed a powder puff. He paused for only a moment before he began to swipe Stayne across his face. Then the Knave grabbed the manequin and threw it over his shoulder. Quickly, the Hatter spun around and grabbed a perfume bottle with a sprayer and, brandishing it, jumped on a chair to bring himself to the same height as the Knave.

"Run, Alice!" the Dormouse called out.

Stayne stopped dead, and the Dormouse recognized her mistake immediately. The Knave looked at Alice, revelation spreading across his face.

"Alice?" he said slowly.

Chapter Thirteen

"RUN!" bellowed the Hatter.

Alice had no choice. She fled out the door with the Knights in hot pursuit.

Stayne's voice boomed down the hall.

"SEIZE HER!"

CHAPTER FOURTEEN

lice burst out into the courtyard with Stayne and the Knights right behind her. She pounded across the cobblestones, but before she could reach the front gate, another squadron of Knights galloped out in front of her.

She skidded to a stop, surrounded by Red Knights on all sides. Alice swung the sword in a circle, keeping them all at a distance. Her hair was tumbling into her face and her makeshift curtain dress kept tripping her as she spun.

Stayne's malevolent chuckle sent a chill down

her spine. Alice turned to face him, holding the sword as threateningly as she could.

"Alice," the Knave sneered. "Of course! Why didn't I see it? Well, it has been a long time." He looked her over from her toes to her large head towering over him. "And you were such a little tyke then." His expression became cold as he held out his hand. "Give me the sword."

"Stay back!" Alice cried, slashing at him. But with her attention focused on Stayne, she didn't see the Knights coming up behind her until two of them had grabbed her arms. She fought and kicked and struggled, never letting go of the sword hilt.

"The Queen will be so pleased," said the Knave. "She'll take great pleasure in taking off your head. I believe she wants to do the deed herself."

One of the Knights wrenched Alice's right arm toward him and reached for the sword.

"*RRRRRRRRRRRRRRRRRRRRRRRRRRRRRRR.*"

A thunderous growl rolled out of the stable door, and suddenly the Bandersnatch leaped out, as bloodthirsty and menacing as ever. Alice flinched and threw herself to the ground, but the monster soared right over her, biting and snapping at the Knights who had held her. Instantly the Knights scattered, yelling in fear.

The Bandersnatch circled back and lowered his head to Alice. It took her a moment to realize what was happening, but as soon as she did, she jumped to her feet and climbed onto his back. His fur was as warm as the bloodhound's, but spikier, as if tiny needles were embedded in it. She clung to his collar with one hand and held the sword aloft with the other as Stayne and the Knights stared, astonished.

The Bandersnatch bolted across the drawbridge and out of the castle. Any Knights standing in their way abandoned their posts with screams of terror. Alice held on tight as they galloped out into the red desert, to freedom.

On a nearby hill, she saw a familiar friend waiting for them.

"Ho, Alice!" he cried, his long ears flapping and his sad face lighting up with startled delight.

"Bayard!" she called. "To Marmoreal!"

The Knave of Hearts breathlessly entered the Red Queen's throne room. He knew this was not going to be a pleasant conversation.

The Red Queen was waiting at the base of her throne, pacing angrily. Her face was fiery red and her fists were clenched. She whirled to glare at the Knave as he walked up to her and bowed.

"Majesty," he said, "Alice has escaped."

In a fury, the Queen slapped him.

"On the Bandersnatch," he added.

She slapped him again. He steeled himself for more.

"With the Vorpal Sword."

The Red Queen slapped him harder than she'd ever slapped him before. He gritted his teeth. The indignities he had to put up with! If only he could be king with no queen anywhere in sight . . .

"How could you let this happen?" she bellowed.

"I may have underestimated her," he admitted, although it pained him to confess such a thing. "But we have her conspirators: the Hatter and the Dormouse."

The Queen's rage seemed to fill the entire great hall.

"OFF WITH THEIR HEADS!"

The White Queen's castle was nothing like her sister's. Where the Red Queen's castle was dark and oppressive, the White Queen's was light and airy.

Sunshine spilled through the open windows, and sweet breezes carried the sound of birds' chattering from outside. A flood of relief coursed through her as she entered the beautiful throne room and saw the Queen sitting on her throne. Everything about her kind face made Alice feel that perhaps this dreadful nightmare would turn out all right in the end.

"Welcome to Marmoreal," said the White Queen, smiling down at Alice and the Vorpal Sword.

"I believe this belongs to you," Alice said. She bowed and held the weapon up for her. The Queen took it with a nod of thanks and strolled gracefully over to the White Knight's shining silver suit of armor, which was set up prominently near the throne. She placed the sword in the suit's hand and turned back to Alice, beaming.

"The Vorpal Sword is home again," she said softly. "The armor is complete. Now all we need is a champion."

The Queen gave Alice a significant look. Alice dropped her eyes and didn't respond. Finally, the Queen went on. "You're a little taller than I thought you'd be."

This Alice did have an answer for. "Blame it on too much *Upelkuchen*," she said, smiling.

"Ah, come with me," said the White Queen, sweeping her long silver robes behind her. Alice followed her down to the kitchen, where delicious smells mingled with the sounds of pots and pans and people singing as they worked.

As they entered, an entire pot of soup was thrown at the door. Alice blinked at the wreckage of the mill. "Is the March Hare here?" she asked, guessing.

"You're late for soup, you wee besom!" bellowed the Hare from across the room. He picked up another pot of soup, and the White Queen ducked. The soup splattered on the door behind Alice. She touched one finger to the wall for a taste.

"It could use salt," she offered.

A saltshaker came flying at her, and Alice ducked to avoid it.

Alice followed the White Queen over to a large cast-iron stove, where a heavy pot full of a curious-smelling liquid was bubbling. The Queen took ingredients from a nearby cupboard, murmuring to herself.

Alice wrinkled her nose, wondering if it might be better if she didn't hear this. She could see a lot of strange-looking things inside the cupboard—ordinary herbs and spices were lined up alongside glass jars of eyeballs and bottles full of shredded insect parts.

The White Queen glanced up at Alice with a smile. "Ah, *pishalver*. Let me think. A pinch of wormfat, urine of the horsefly, buttered fingers . . ." Her face turned thoughtful again as she reached back into the cupboard. "My sister preferred to study Dominion Over Living Things. Tell me, how does she seem to you?"

"Perfectly horrid," Alice answered truthfully.

"And her head?"

"Bulbous," said Alice.

"I think she may have some kind of growth in there . . . something pressing on her brain," the White Queen said, shaking her head sadly. "Three coins from a dead man's pocket, two tablespoons of wishful thinking . . ."

"You can't imagine the things that go on in that place," Alice blurted. She couldn't understand how the White Queen could sit here, calmly making potions and discussing theories, while her subjects suffered so much under the Red Queen.

"Oh, yes, I can," the Queen assured her. "But when a champion steps forth to slay the Jabberwocky, the people will rise against her." She leaned over and sniffed the nasty concoction in the pot, then spit into it. "That should do it."

The White Queen fished a spoon out of a drawer, dipped it in the potion, and offered it to Alice. "Blow," she cautioned her.

Alice blew on the potion to cool it off, then took a sip. She knew better than to drink too much this time. Within a moment, she had shrunk to her normal size—or at least, she felt normal next to the White Queen, so she seemed right to herself. She wondered how she would measure up out in the real world, if she ever got back there.

"Feel better?" asked the Queen.

"Much," said Alice.

The Queen replaced the spoon in the pot and dusted her hands off, looking suddenly official and businesslike. "There's someone here who would like to speak with you."

CHAPTER FIFTEEN

Down in the depths of the Red Queen's dungeons, the Hatter was slumped on the floor of a cold cell, staring off into space. Mallymkun was trapped inside a large birdcage hanging from the ceiling. She clung to the wiry iron bars and gazed at him, but he was beyond her reach at the moment, both physically and emotionally.

She peered into the cell across the way, where a female bloodhound named Bielle was pacing around her shivering pups, trying desperately to warm them. Mallymkun was fairly certain she recognized her as Bayard's wife, but Bielle was too upset to stop and talk with the Dormouse long enough to confirm it.

Just then, the clomp of heavy footsteps on the dungeon stairs announced the arrival of Stayne and his Red Knights. Bielle whirled and stared at the approaching guards, although they ignored her and her pups.

"Hatter!" barked the Knave, banging on the bars of the cage. There was no response. The Hatter continued to stare blindly into space.

One of the Knights reached through the bars and prodded the Hatter with his truncheon. When there was still no response, the Knight offered, "He's gone off the deep end." This was the usual opinion of the Hatter, so it surprised no one.

"Pity," said the Knave. He folded his arms and smirked. "It is a bore to behead a madman. No weeping, no begging . . ." He cast a meaningful look at the dogs in the opposite cage. Bielle hurled herself against the bars, her large brown eyes pleading.

"Why are you keeping us here?" she cried. "We've done nothing wrong!"

"Madam, blame your husband," Stayne said with a snort. "He left you here to rot."

"You lie!" howled the bloodhound, throwing herself at the bars with new fury and snarling at the Knights. Stayne jumped back out of her reach, and in an instant, the Hatter was up and at the bars, seizing Stayne and pulling him back against the cage. His arm went around Stayne's neck, and he began to squeeze, choking the life out of him.

There was madness in the Hatter's eyes, and he clearly felt no pain as Stayne struggled. Finally Stayne staggered free, gasping.

The Knave clawed at his neck, struggling for air, and when he could finally breathe, he pointed at the Hatter with hatred in his eyes. "Your head comes off at dawn! And that one, too!" He jabbed a finger toward the Dormouse.

The Hatter shrugged and spread his hands in a concilitory gesture.

"Have a pleasant night," he sneered, then spun on his heel and led his Knights out of the dungeon.

The unspoken words were clear to the prisoners: *It will be your last.*

The White Queen escorted Alice out of the castle to the topiary garden. Alice felt restless and worried. As horrible as it was, she wished she were back at the Red Queen's castle, just so she could know what was happening with the Hatter. Was he still alive? Were they beating him again? What did he think of her escaping and leaving him to suffer whatever punishment the Queen would throw at him?

Guilt tugged at her heart as she rounded a curve in the hedge maze. Just ahead, lit up by the moonlight, she spotted a topiary mushroom, neat curves and edges sliced out of the shrubbery. A telltale plume of smoke was rising from the top.

"Absolem?" Alice asked, walking up to it.

The large blue Caterpillar raised his head from his hookah and peered at her. "Who are you?" he asked through a cloud of smoke.

Alice nearly smiled. "I thought we'd settled this. I'm Alice . . . but not *that* one."

"How do you know?" Absolem asked serenely. He blew smoke in her face and she coughed, waving it away.

"You said so yourself," she pointed out.

"I said you were Not Hardly Alice," he corrected her. "But you're much more her now. In fact, you're Almost Alice."

"Even so," said Alice, shaking her head, "I couldn't slay the Jabberwocky if my life depended on it."

"It will," the Caterpillar said matter-of-factly.

"So I suggest you keep the Vorpal Sword on hand when the Frabjous Day arrives."

Fed up and curious, Alice reached out and poked the Caterpillar's jiggly blue belly. His eyes nearly popped out with surprise.

"No touching!" he yelped. "There's no touching!"

"You seem so real," Alice said thoughtfully. "Sometimes I forget that this is all a dream."

The Caterpillar blew smoke in her face again, as if he thought that was the only appropriate response to such a remark.

"Will you stop doing that!" Alice protested, waving the smoke away. Absolem began to chuckle, sending ripples of mirth along his entire round body. She could still hear him chuckling as the smoke enveloped him, hiding him from view, and she turned to walk back into the night.

Back in the Red Queen's dungeon, the Hatter was

dusting off his hat and trying to get his sad clothes to perk up. He didn't want to go to his execution looking like a disheveled mess.

"I've always admired that hat," purred a smooth voice from outside the bars.

The Hatter looked up and saw the Cheshire Cat lounging against the stone wall. His eyes narrowed. "Hello, Chess."

The Cat's tail whisked back and forth. He stroked one of his long whiskers and studied the Hatter's efforts to rehabilitate his outfit. "Since you won't be needing it anymore," he said after a moment, "would you consider bequeathing it to me?"

The Hatter touched his beloved hat and raised his chin with dignity. "How dare you! It is a formal execution. I want to look my best, you know."

The Cheshire Cat fell silent for another minute. Finally he sighed. "It's a pity about all this. I was looking forward to seeing you *Futterwacken*."

"I was rather good at it, was I not?" said the Hatter ruefully.

The Cheshire Cat's feline eyes glowed intently. "I really do love that hat," he purred. "I would wear it to all the finest occasions."

His eyes met the Hatter's, and they stared at each other for a long, thoughtful moment.

Hours later, the Hatter and the Dormouse, their heads bowed in resignation, were marched out of the cell and down the long walk to the executioner's platform. A crowd was gathered in the outside courtyard to watch them pass, including the White Rabbit and the Tweedles, who stared at the prisoners with glum faces. The Queen watched from a high balcony, ignoring the misery on the faces of the crowd.

"I love a morning execution. Don't you?" the Queen said.

"Yes, Your Majesty," the courtiers responded all together.

The Hatter stepped forward first, pushing the Dormouse behind him. The burly executioner loomed over them both, his face hidden by the usual thick executioner's mask. The Hatter rested his head on the beheading stone. The executioner reached for the Hatter's tophat, and the Hatter leaned away from him.

"I'd like to keep it on," he mumbled.

The executioner shrugged. "Suit yourself," he said. "As long as I can get at your neck." The executioner moved the hat's ribbons away from the Hatter's neck.

"I'm right behind you," the Dormouse squeaked bravely.

"Off with his head!" the Red Queen bellowed.

The White Rabbit covered his eyes. "I can't watch," he moaned.

The executioner raised his sword high into the air. The morning sun gleamed off the sharp edge. A frightened hush fell over the crowd, and in the silence they could all hear the zip of the sword as it flashed down, followed by a *CLANG* as it hit the stone where the Hatter's neck had been.

Everyone gasped, including the Queen and Stayne.

The Hatter's head . . .

. . . had *disappeared*.

CHAPTER SIXTEEN

The sound of the sword hitting the stone was still reverberating through the courtyard. The executioner stepped back, wincing and touching his muscles where the shock had jarred him.

The Tweedles stared at each other in disbelief, almost daring one another to disagree about what had just happened.

Then, the Rabbit looked up. Before him was what looked like a floating head, with no body attached at all. Then it all became clear. It was the Cheshire Cat's disembodied head wearing the Hatter's hat!

He hovered there before them all and grinned. "Good morning, everyone!"

"Chess, you dog!" the Dormouse cried in delight.

He winked at her. The sound of the Hatter's familiar laugh drifted across the courtyard, and everyone turned to find him perched on a balustrade near the Queen's courtiers.

"Madam," the Hatter called cheerfully. "You are being heinously bamboozled by these lickspittle toadies you surround yourself with!" He reached out and tugged lightly on Lady Long Ears' nearest ear. It promptly came off in his hand, and Lady Long Ears screamed. The Hatter held up the ear and the Red Queen squinted at it from her balcony.

"What is that?" she demanded.

Terrified, Lady Long Ears lashed out to defend herself. "I'm not the only one, Majesty," she shrieked. "Look!" She grabbed the enormous nose of the woman beside her and pulled. It came off with a noisy *squck*, revealing her real, ordinary-size nose underneath.

"A counterfeit nose!" blustered Big Belly Man. "You should be ashamed!"

"Me?" Lady Large Nose yelled. "What about that big belly you're so proud of?" Before he could escape her prying hands, she grabbed his shirt and pulled it up to reveal his fake belly. As the Hatter had expected, they were remarkably quick to turn on each other.

And as he'd also expected, the Red Queen was mightily displeased to find her courtiers were conspiring against her. In fact, she was nearly apoplectic with rage by this point. "Liars! Cheats! Falsifiers! Off with their heads!"

Pandemonium broke out. The Hatter leaped to a high ledge and called to the creatures below. "To the abused and enslaved of the Red Queen's court, stand up and fight! Rise up against the bloody Red Queen!"

Monkeys threw off their tabletops and chair seats, screeching their defiance. A frog holding a tray of tarts tossed them up into the air. Birds dropped their lamps and coasted down to land on their legs, resting their exhausted wings. All across the courtyard and inside the palace, creatures threw off their bonds and took up the battle cry.

"*Downal wyth Bluddy Behg Hid!*" they shouted. The phrase echoed off the flagstones and filled the morning air. "*Downal wyth Bluddy Behg Hid!*"

Infuriated, the Red Queen clutched the balcony railing and stamped her foot. "RELEASE THE JUBJUB BIRD!" she screamed.

A bloodcurdling screech cut through the cries of defiance as the JubJub Bird swooped down from his aerie. He clawed and snapped indiscriminately, sowing death through the panicked onlookers below. The Queen watched with a vengeful smile.

"You're right, Stayne," she said fiercely. "It is far better to be feared than loved."

But what she did not see in the chaos below was a small crowd, including the Hatter, the Dormouse, the White Rabbit, and the Tweedles, gathering to escape.

"Come boys, quickly," the Hatter called.

"Hatter!" said the Dormouse.

"Come on, Mally. Quickly! Come on! Come on!" he responded.

They darted away from the JubJub Bird's death-dealing talons and made for the drawbridge . . . and freedom.

"Prepare the Jabberwocky for battle," the Queen commanded. "We're going to visit my little sister."

CHAPTER SEVENTEEN

On the other side of Underland, Alice stood on the parapet of the White Queen's castle with Bayard and the White Queen. They were watching the stars come out in the evening sky, each with their own growing sense of unease.

"I had hoped to have a champion by now," the White Queen said, a little pointedly.

"Why don't you slay the Jabberwocky yourself?" Alice asked. "You must have the power," she said.

"In the healing arts," said the Queen, shaking her head. "It is against my vows to bring harm to any living creature," she added with a hint of melodrama in her voice. Alice shrugged and looked back out at the landscape below. The Queen spotted a hideous bug flying near her face, and swiped it away, then pretended to pirouette so as not to be caught breaking her "vow."

Then something caught the Queen's eye in the distance. She lifted her spyglass.

"We have company," she said, handing her spyglass to Alice.

Alice focused the spyglass on the bluffs. Her heart leaped as she saw the Hatter, the Dormouse, and a host of other creatures running over the rise. They were safe! She hadn't left them to die after all!

She also spotted something else. "Have a look, Bayard," she said.

The bloodhound's long ears drooped on either side of the instrument as he peered through. It took him a moment, but finally he spotted the female bloodhound and pups who were running with the rest of them.

"Bielle!" he cried, overwhelmed with joy. He spun around to race down to the entrance courtyard, and Alice followed him, her golden hair flying out behind her as she ran.

Bayard reached the courtyard first, just as the group came across the drawbridge. He galloped up to his wife and pups, and they all leaped around, whinnying and nuzzling each other joyfully. The White Rabbit pressed his paws together with delight.

The Tweedles rushed to the White Queen, who was happy to see them. She kissed each of them, leaving lipstick marks on their foreheads.

Alice's eyes went straight to the Hatter. His clothes were bright and happy, reflecting the delight on his face. She ran up and threw her arms around him. "I'm so happy to see you!" she cried. "I thought they were going to—"

"So did I!" he interrupted her enthusiastically. "But they didn't." His voice started to speed up again, and he clutched her hands as if he might never let go. "And now, here I am . . . still in one piece . . . and I'm rather glad about that now that I'm seeing you again . . . I would have regretted not seeing you again . . . especially now that you're you and the proper size . . . and it's a good size . . . it's a great size . . . it's a right-proper Alice size . . ."

"Hatter," Alice said kindly. He snapped back into the moment.

"Size, Fez . . . I'm fine," he said, blinking strange eyes at her. And it was true, he *was* fine, even though Alice had been afraid she'd never see him again. She felt too full of happiness to say what she really wanted to.

"Where's your hat?" she asked. She curiously touched his curly red hair.

They both jumped as the top hat suddenly

materialized in the air beside them, followed slowly by the head of the Cheshire Cat underneath it, then the rest of him.

"Chessur?" Alice said.

"How's the arm, luv?" the Cat purred.

"All healed," she said, showing him how the swelling had gone down. The scratches were already almost entirely gone.

The Hatter held out his hand for the hat, and the Cheshire Cat reluctantly returned it. "Good-bye, sweet hat," he murmured.

As the Hatter replaced it in its rightful place on his head, he glanced at Alice again, and they shared a smile that said more than any words could have.

Night had fallen again, and the escaped creatures from the Red Queen's castle were safely tucked away in various corners of the White Queen's home.

Up on a high tower, beneath the stars, Alice sat with the Hatter, their legs swinging over a long drop below.

"Have you any idea why a raven's like a writing desk?" the Hatter asked dreamily.

"Let me think about it!" Alice said, smiling.

He shifted to gaze into her eyes. "You know what tomorrow is, don't you?" he said.

"Frabjous Day," Alice said with a sigh. The whole castle had been murmuring and whispering and chattering about it all day. "How could I forget? I wish I'd wake up!"

The Hatter looked bemused. "You still believe this is a dream? Do you?"

"Of course. This has all come from my own mind."

The Hatter thought about that for a moment. "Which would mean that *I'm* not real."

"I'm afraid so," said Alice, shaking her head.

"You're just a figment of my imagination. I *would* dream up someone who's half mad."

"Yes, yes. But you would have to be half mad to dream me up," the Hatter observed.

"I must be, then," Alice said.

Alice laughed.

"I'll miss you when I wake up," she said.

Chapter Eighteen

The next morning, everyone gathered in the White Queen's courtyard at dawn. A sense of fear and exhilaration filled the air. This was the Frabjous Day. Today everything would change . . . but whether for better or for worse, no one could say.

The White Rabbit drew out a gleaming gold trumpet and sounded a summoning call that hushed the milling crowd.

"Who will step forth to be champion for the White Queen?" he cried.

"That would be I!" said the Mad Hatter, stepping forward valiantly.

The Cheshire Cat snorted. "You have very poor evaporating skills. I should be the one."

"No, me!" cried Tweedledum.

"No, *me!*" shouted Tweedledee, pushing his brother behind him.

The White Rabbit held up the Oraculum and the illustration of Alice slaying the Jabberwocky. Everyone fell quiet.

"No other slayer, no-how," murmured Tweedledum.

"If it ain't Alice, it ain't dead," agreed Tweedledee.

All the eyes in the courtyard turned to Alice. The weight of their gazes, all their expectations, reminded her of the pressure she felt under the gazebo as Hamish proposed marriage to her with the entire garden party looking on.

"Alice," said the White Queen, "you cannot live your life to please others. The choice must be yours because when you step out to face that creature, you will step out alone."

Alice stared at the picture of the horrible monster that was winging its way toward them. She saw her golden hair flying as she wielded the Vorpal Sword, but she still couldn't imagine how it would feel—the thunk of the blade slicing into flesh, the scrape of its long sharp claws against her pale skin. She was not a killer. How could she kill anything . . . let alone Underland's most dreaded creature?

Overwhelmed, Alice turned and ran out of the courtyard. She bolted through the castle and out into the gardens until she found the hedge maze, where she threw herself onto a garden bench and wept.

"Nothing was ever accomplished with tears," observed a voice. Alice lifted her tear-streaked face and looked around.

"Absolem?"

She peered at the nearest hedge and saw him hanging upside down on a leaf, spinning a silvery green web around himself.

"Why are you upside down?" she asked.

"I've come to the end of this life," he explained calmly.

Alice didn't know why she felt so upset; she barely knew him. "You're going to die?" she said.

"Transform," he answered, although it wasn't much of an answer. The web already covered half of his body.

"Don't go," Alice pleaded. "I need your help. I don't know what to do!"

"I can't help you if you don't even know who you are, stupid girl."

Now Alice was angry. "I'm not stupid! My name is Alice. I live in London. I have a mother named Helen and a sister named Margaret. My father was Charles Kingsleigh. He had a vision that stretched halfway around the world, and nothing ever stopped him. He probably would have liked it here." She paused, realizing what she was saying. It felt like an epiphany dawning upon her. All she needed was her father's strength and vision and faith in himself. Slowly she said, "I'm his daughter. I'm Alice Kingsleigh."

"Alice at last!" cried the Caterpillar. "You were just as dim-witted the first time you were here. You called it 'Wonderland,' as I recall."

"Wonderland . . ." Alice echoed. Her dream came flooding back with all of its details. Young Alice in Wonderland . . . Alice in the room of doors, Alice with the Cheshire Cat, Alice at the mad tea party . . . Alice with the Red Queen and Playing Cards, painting the roses red . . . young Alice with the Caterpillar . . .

"It wasn't a dream at all!" Alice burst out. "It was a memory! This place is real! And so are you." Her heart leaped. "And so is the Hatter."

"And the Jabberwocky," the Caterpillar reminded her. "Remember, the Vorpal Sword knows what it wants. All you have to do is hold on to it. *Fairfarren*, Alice. Perhaps I will see you in another life."

He disappeared inside the green chrysalis, swallowed up even more thoroughly than he'd vanished into his clouds of smoke.

Alice sat for a moment, thinking. Finally she got to her feet and wiped away the last traces of her tears.

She knew what she had to do.

The Red Queen's army marched steadily across the Crimson Desert, red banners fluttering high over their heads. The Queen rode in the lead on a black charger, the Knave of Hearts at her side. The JubJub Bird flew ahead, and far above them, a monstrous winged shadow soared.

On they came, unstoppable, formidable, and terrifying.

The mood in the White Queen's courtyard was somber. Without Alice, how could they have any chance of winning the coming battle? The Tweedles stood with their arms around each other, heads bowed in despair. The March Hare wrung his paws and ears, his eyes darting nervously from side to side.

The Mad Hatter leaned against the wall, waiting. He knew Alice. He believed in her. He refused to give up hope.

Suddenly there was a resounding clatter from inside the castle. The Bandersnatch loped out into the courtyard, drool dripping from its squashed bulldog face. A White Knight rode on his back, and for a moment the eyes of the crowd were dazzled by the sun gleaming off the shiny silver armor.

Then they saw the blond hair hanging down from the helmet, and the Vorpal Sword raised high in Alice's hand. A rousing cheer rose from the crowd . . . their champion had arrived.

CHAPTER NINETEEN

The clearing in the wood was still black and covered in ash from the last encounter. The White Queen's people approached in silence, the heavy weight of their sad history hanging over them. Alice glanced at the Hatter, her heart aching for him as she thought of all the family he had lost here.

The Red Queen waited on her steed, a malevolent smile plastered across her enormous face. Her eyes glittered with hatred as her sister rode into the clearing.

"Hello, Iracebeth," said the White Queen, pulling her white horse to a halt.

"Hello, Mirana," said the Red Queen coldly.

The White Rabbit blew his trumpet and unrolled a scroll. "On this, the Frabjous Day," he announced, "the queens, Red and White, shall send forth their champions to do battle on their behalf."

The White Queen stared into her sister's eyes, tears trembling on her beautiful long lashes. "Oh, 'Racie," she said.

The Red Queen's eyes softened at the sound of her childhood nickname.

"We don't have to fight," the White Queen went on.

The Red Queen snapped her mouth shut and glared suspiciously. "I know what you're doing," she snarled. "You think you can blink those pretty little eyes and I'll melt like Mummy and Daddy did."

The White Queen held out her smooth white arms beseechingly. "Please," she said sweetly.

"It's *my* crown!" screamed the Red Queen. "*I'm*

the eldest! JABBERWOCKY!" Her horse pranced and spun, feeling the bolt of terror that shot through the crowd as an enormous dark form rose up behind the Red Queen.

The Jabberwocky's vast wingspan blocked out the sun and darkened the clearing. It swung its reptilian head, studying them all with small, glistening eyes. Its long, spiked tail whipped across the grass. It extended one long, deadly claw and adjusted its red vest.

Alice could barely contain her fear. "This is impossible," she whispered to the Hatter, standing loyally beside her foot.

"Only if you believe it is," said the Mad Hatter. He looked up into her eyes, and his words sparked a memory of her father.

"Sometimes I believe as many as six impossible things before breakfast," Alice said, smiling down at him.

"That is an excellent practice," the Hatter agreed. "However, just at the moment, you really might want to focus on the Jabberwocky."

That was the right answer. Alice slid off the Bandersnatch, tossed back her hair, and adjusted the sword at her waist. She was ready.

"Where's your champion, sister?" the Red Queen sneered.

"Here," said Alice, stepping boldly into the clearing.

"Hello, Um," the Red Queen said.

The Jabberwocky hissed with pleasure. He slithered toward her, opened his slavering jaw, and roared.

"Six impossible things," Alice whispered to herself, her voice trembling. "Count them, Alice. One! There's a potion that can make you shrink. Two! And a cake that can make you grow."

She drew the Vorpal Sword. The Jabberwocky lowered its huge head and loomed over her.

"Sssso, my old foe," it hissed in a horrible voice that made Alice's skin feel like it was crawling with insects. "We meet on the battlefield once again."

Alice was shocked. She hadn't known the Jabberwocky could talk . . . and she was sure she'd remember if they'd ever met in battle before. She couldn't possibly have blocked out that part of her earlier visit, could she?

"We've never met," she said, hoping he couldn't hear the wavering in her voice.

"Not you, insignificant bearer," said the Jabberwocky, casting her a scornful glance. "My ancient enemy, the Vorpal one."

"That's enough chatter!" Alice commanded.

Suddenly the Jabberwocky's spiked tongue shot out toward the sword. Startled, Alice flung the sword up to defend herself, and it sliced right through the Jabberwocky's tongue. The tongue flopped to the ground, wriggling in the dirt. Alice stepped back out of its way with a look of disgust. Now all the Jabberwocky could do was burble incoherently.

Alice was feeling triumphant when the Jabberwocky's pronged tail whipped around and knocked her to the ground. Alice barely kept her grip on the Vorpal Sword, and her breath was knocked out of her. She lay still for a moment, gasping.

"Three," she said aloud to herself. "Animals can talk."

Some instinct made her roll out of the way just as the Jabberwocky's tail slammed down to impale her.

"Four," she said, faltering. "Four, Alice!" She climbed to her feet. "Cats can disappear.

"Five. There is a place called Wonderland," she said firmly. The Jabberwocky swiped at her with long, curved claws, and she deflected them with a *clang* of her sword.

"Six," Alice said, taking a deep breath. She stood

still for a moment, then slowly lifted her head. All the fear was gone. There was nothing but fierce intention in her eyes. She knew the sixth impossible thing . . . and she believed it.

"I can slay the Jabberwocky!" she cried. She swung the sword in a wide arc and attacked with fury. Surprised by her fierceness, the Jabberwocky jumped back, then lashed out in defense. Now the battle had really begun.

Alice whirled, distracted, and claws scraped down the back of her armor. The Hatter winced. Alice backed up toward the Hatter, fending off the Jabberwocky.

"The Hatter's interfering!" howled the Red Queen. "Off with his head!"

The Knave of Hearts drew his sword and ran at the Mad Hatter, who promptly drew his own sword to fight back. The well-ordered duel between champions erupted into a full-scale battle, with

Alice and the Jabberwocky at the eye of the storm.

Mallymkun leaped onto Bayard's back, Bielle growling fiercely at his side. Together, the bloodhounds and the Dormouse leaped at the JubJub Bird, wielding teeth and hatpins against its deadly talons.

The Cheshire Cat appeared in front of a Red Knight, then vanished as a sword was thrust at his middle. Confused, the Knight spun around and tried again, but the Cat could not be cornered.

With a howl, the Bandersnatch attacked four Red Knights at once, his strong jaws snapping around their armor. Meanwhile, the Tweedles fought back-to-back, with perfect precision and timing and nary a single argument. Not far away, the March Hare managed to shake off his paralyzing fear and started flinging anything he could find like a wild man, knocking out Red Knights right and left.

But the crux of the battle was still between Alice and the Jabberwocky, and she didn't have time to watch her friends to make sure they were all right.

Alice attacked the beast with fierce thrust, swipes, and uppercuts. But the Jabberwocky was no easy opponent. It swiped back, and Alice was hit! The Vorpal Sword was knocked out of her hand, and she landed with a grunt at the bottom of a staircase. She quickly picked up the sword and ran up the stairs, where the battle continued. The Jabberwocky's long, scaly neck snaked past her for barely a moment, and she seized the opportunity to leap onto his back, pulling herself up his sharp, bumpy scales. She could feel the edges of the scales cutting into the armored gloves on her hands. The Jabberwocky twisted and snapped, trying to shake her off.

The Vorpal Sword nearly wrenched itself out of Alice's hand in its relentless pursuit of the creature's head. Alice could barely keep her grip on it. She threw herself into the air.

"OFF WITH *YOUR* HEAD!" she yelled.

With one powerful thrust, Alice sank the Vorpal Sword into the Jabberwocky's neck, severing its head from its vile body. The head rolled down the stairs and landed at the feet of the Red Queen.

Alice was too exhausted to speak, but the dead creature's head seemed to say everything.

The Queen pointed at Alice imperiously.

"KILL HER!" she bellowed.

CHAPTER TWENTY

There was a long, tense pause as the battling stopped all around the clearing. Alice stared at the Red Queen's finger, which was only inches from her neck. She was still breathing too hard to speak.

The nearest Red Knight tossed his sword down on the ground. "We follow you no more," he said to the Red Queen, "Bloody Big Head."

"How dare you!" shrieked Iracebeth. "Off with his head!"

Another Red Knight threw down his sword, then another, and another, and gradually every single

Knight in the clearing disarmed himself, staring defiantly at the Red Queen. She stamped her feet furiously, and then her shrieks of rage grew even louder as the crown lifted off her head and started to float through the air. Iracebeth grabbed for it, but it wafted out of her reach and over to Mirana, where it settled gently on the White Queen's head.

"Iracebeth of Crims," said the White Queen, "your crimes against Underland are worthy of death. However, that is against my vows. Therefore, you are banished to the Outlands. No one is to show you any kindness or ever speak a word to you. You will have not a friend in the world."

The Knave of Hearts sidled up to the White Queen and bowed unctuously. "Majesty," he said in his slippery, slimy voice, "I hope you bear me no ill will."

"Only this one," Mirana said, pointing without looking at him. "Ilosovic Stayne, you will join

Chapter Twenty

Iracebeth in banishment from this day until the end of Underland."

The Knave went very pale. Knights seized his arms and chained him to Iracebeth. The former Red Queen leaned toward him, batting her giant eyes. "At least we have each other," she said.

In a panic, Stayne pulled out a knife and tried to stab Iracebeth. She screamed as the Hatter threw a pair of scissors and knocked the knife away. Stayne dropped to his knees before the White Queen.

"Majesty, please kill me . . ." he begged. "Please."

"But I do not owe you a kindness," the White Queen said, looking down at him with no pity in her eyes.

"Take off my head!" he pleaded.

Knights dragged the unfortunate pair away. As they vanished into the woods, everyone could still hear Iracebeth screaming at Stayne. "You tried to kill me! HE TRIED TO KILL ME! He tried to kill me!"

Her voice faded into the distance, and a soft breeze seemed to send a sigh of relief through everyone in the clearing. All at once, the Hatter burst into an enthusiastic dance.

"Oh, the Frabjous Day!" he sang out happily. "Calloo! Callay!"

"What is he doing?" asked Alice, amused. She had taken off some pieces of her heavy armor and was breathing more easily now.

"*Futterwacken*," the Cheshire Cat answered her, grinning.

The White Queen knelt beside the body of the fallen Jabberwocky and caught a drop of its blood in a vial. She stood up and handed the vial to Alice as the Hatter let her go.

"And blood of the Jabberwocky," said the Queen. "You have our everlasting gratitude. And for your efforts on our behalf, I give you this."

The Queen handed the vial to Alice. She held it up to the light, surprised by the color of the blood inside. "Will this take me home?" she asked.

"If that is what you choose," said the Queen.

Alice lifted the vial, but stopped as the Hatter put his hand on hers.

"You could stay," he said, his gaze warm and full of promise.

"What an idea," Alice said softly. "A crazy, mad, wonderful idea." She looked around at all the strange and wonderful beings she'd met in this and wonderfully strange place. She imagined what it would be like to stay—to talk to animals every day, to ride the Bandersnatch and explore Underland, to dance the *Futterwacken* with the Hatter whenever she chose.

But thoughts of her mother and sister and unfinished business intruded, and she knew she could not stay . . . at least, not now.

"But I can't," she said to the Hatter, taking his hand. "There are questions I have to answer. Things I have to do."

She poured the new potion into her mouth. "I'll be back again before you know it," she promised the Hatter.

"You won't remember me."

"Of course I will!" she said. "How could I forget? Hatter . . . why *is* a raven like a writing desk?"

"I haven't the slightest idea. *Fairfarren*, Alice."

All of Underland began to shimmer around him, and his hand disappeared from hers as everything dissolved into—

—the meadow where Alice had first chased the White Rabbit. Alice found herself clinging to the edge of a rabbit hole. She pulled herself up and out of the hole. Grass was tangled in her long hair, and her clothes were wrinkled and torn. She shook her head, trying to remember what had happened. How odd. Had she fallen asleep?

She stood up and brushed off her skirts.

Whether she wanted to or not, she thought, she'd better get back to Hamish and the party.

Chapter Twenty-one

The garden party was still going on at the Ascot estate, although the guests were rather subdued after the failed proposal. Most of them stood in clumps across the great lawn, whispering in bewilderment.

Hamish spoke to some of the confused guests, his sideburns wrinkling as he complained. "She left me standing there without an answer," he whined.

"A case of nerves, no doubt," said Fiona reassuringly.

Suddenly, silence fell as Alice wandered back onto the lawn. Everyone stared in shock at her disheveled appearance. She looked as if she'd been through a great battle.

"Alice?" said Hamish.

"Good lord," said Lord Ascot. "Are you all right?"

Alice's mother hurried to her, gently taking her arm. "What happened to you?" Helen Kingsleigh asked, worried.

—"I fell down a hole and hit my head," Alice answered, although she couldn't help but feel that she was missing some part of the story.

"You look a frightful mess," Lady Ascot sniffed.

Alice turned to Hamish. Her adventures in Underland were gone from her memory, but the self-confidence remained. And there was a lot she needed to say.

"I'm sorry, Hamish," she said. "I can't marry you. You're not the right man for me. And there's that trouble with your digestion." She turned to her sister. "I love you, Margaret. But this is my life.

I'll decide what to do with it." Her sister's husband was standing next to Margaret, twitching nervously. "You're lucky to have my sister for your wife, Lowell. I know you'll be good to her. I'll be watching very closely."

Lowell blanched at her veiled threat. Alice went on to her aunt Imogene. "There is no prince, Aunt Imogene. You need to talk to someone about these delusions." Her chin went up as she faced Lady Ascot. "I happen to love rabbits," she said, "especially white ones."

Lady Ascot looked disapproving, but she didn't say anything as Alice turned to her mother and kissed her on the cheek. "Don't worry, Mother. I'll find something useful to do with my life."

Helen squeezed her hand, smiling through proud tears. Alice had never reminded her more of her dear Charles.

Alice noticed the Chattaway sisters hovering

nearby. "You two remind me of some funny boys I met in a dream," she said with a grin. She looked around. Was there anyone else she meant to speak to?

Lord Ascot lifted a finger. "You've left me out," he said.

"No, I haven't, sir," said Alice. "You and I have business to discuss."

"Shall we speak in the study?" He took her elbow to lead her away, but Alice turned back for a moment.

"Oh, and one more thing," she said. She lifted her skirts above her ankles and did a brisky, happy *Futterwacken* to the shock of some and the delight of others. Then she calmly followed Lord Ascot into his mansion.

Maps were spread across Lord Ascot's desk, along with ledgers and other documents of the business he had taken over from Charles Kingsleigh. Alice leaned over a map of the world.

"My father told me he planned to expand his trade route to Sumatra and Borneo," she said, tracing the outlines of the exotic countries with her finger. "But I don't think he was looking far enough."

"Not far enough?" said Lord Ascot, astonished.

"Why not go all the way to China?" Alice asked. "It's vast, the culture is rich, and we have a foothold in Hong Kong. To be the first to trade with China. Can you imagine it?"

She looked up at him. Her eyes were shining just like her father's had.

Lord Ascot smiled. "You know, if anybody else had said that to me, I'd say, 'You've lost your senses.' But I've seen that look before. As you're not going to be my daughter-in-law, perhaps you would consider becoming an apprentice with the company?"

Six months later, Alice stood on the deck of a China Trading Company ship, waving to her mother, sister, and Lord Ascot on the dock below. White sails billowed overhead as the ship pulled out into the ocean, and Alice felt the wind lift her hair into a wild dance of freedom around her head.

A beautiful monarch butterfly with blue-tinged wings landed on her shoulder. She smiled, one memory breaking through as clear as day.

"Hello, Absolem," she said.

The butterfly took wing, and Alice watched it soar away into the sky with a smile of pure joy on her face.

THE END

The Sleeping Beauty

Retold by Margaret Nash

Illustrated by Barbara Vagnozzi

FRANKLIN WATTS
LONDON•SYDNEY

Once upon a time a
beautiful princess was born.

The happy King and
Queen gave a feast.

They invited all the good
fairies in the land.

Each fairy gave the princess
a gift: beauty, kindness and
all good things.

The last fairy was just
waiting to give her gift ...

.... when a wicked fairy
flew in. "So you didn't
invite me!" she snarled.

"Well, when that baby is fifteen she will prick her finger on a spindle and die!"

"I cannot break the spell,
but I can make it better,"
said the good fairy.

12

"The princess will not die,
but she will sleep for a
hundred years."

The King and Queen
burned all the spindles
in the land.

Fifteen years passed.

On her fifteenth birthday,
the princess climbed up a
tower she had never
visited before.

Inside, an old lady was
spinning. "Please, let me
try," said the princess.

She picked up the spindle.
"OW!" she cried. She'd
pricked her finger!

The princess fell asleep.

Everyone else in the
castle fell asleep, too!

Years passed by. A thorn
hedge grew up around
the castle. Nobody
could get through.

After a hundred years, a
prince came to the castle.
The thorns parted.

The prince got into the
courtyard ...

... through the hall ...

.... and up to the tower.

There he found the
beautiful sleeping princess.
He woke her with a kiss.

Everyone else woke up, too!

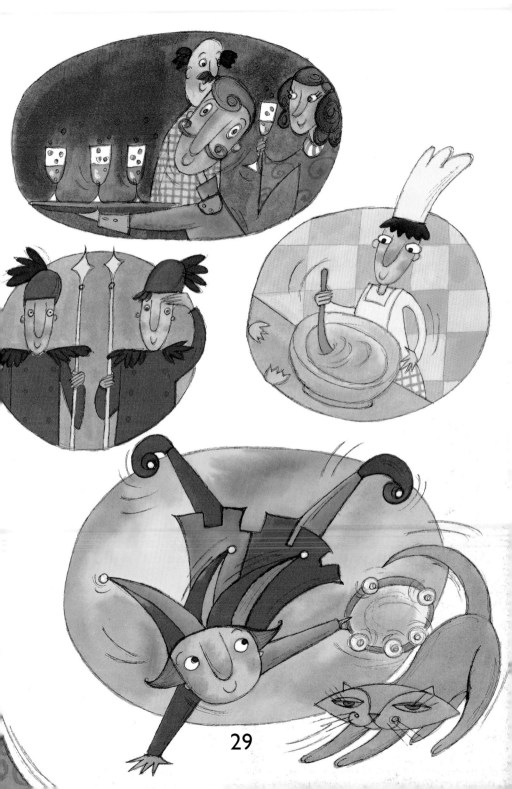

The prince married the
beautiful princess.

And they lived happily
ever after.

Leapfrog has been specially designed to fit the requirements of the National Literacy Strategy. It offers real books for beginning readers by top authors and illustrators.

There are 31 Leapfrog stories to choose from:

The Bossy Cockerel
Written by Margaret Nash,
illustrated by Elisabeth Moseng

Bill's Baggy Trousers
Written by Susan Gates,
illustrated by Anni Axworthy

Mr Spotty's Potty
Written by Hilary Robinson,
illustrated by Peter Utton

Little Joe's Big Race
Written by Andy Blackford,
illustrated by Tim Archbold

The Little Star
Written by Deborah Nash,
illustrated by Richard Morgan

The Cheeky Monkey
Written by Anne Cassidy,
illustrated by Lisa Smith

Selfish Sophie
Written by Damian Kelleher,
illustrated by Georgie Birkett

Recycled!
Written by Jillian Powell,
illustrated by Amanda Wood

Felix on the Move
Written by Maeve Friel,
illustrated by Beccy Blake

Pippa and Poppa
Written by Anne Cassidy,
illustrated by Philip Norman

Jack's Party
Written by Ann Bryant,
illustrated by Claire Henley

The Best Snowman
Written by Margaret Nash,
illustrated by Jörg Saupe

Eight Enormous Elephants
Written by Penny Dolan,
illustrated by Leo Broadley

Mary and the Fairy
Written by Penny Dolan,
illustrated by Deborah Allwright

The Crying Princess
Written by Anne Cassidy,
illustrated by Colin Paine

Jasper and Jess
Written by Anne Cassidy,
illustrated by François Hall

The Lazy Scarecrow
Written by Jillian Powell,
illustrated by Jayne Coughlin

The Naughty Puppy
Written by Jillian Powell,
illustrated by Summer Durantz

Freddie's Fears
Written by Hilary Robinson,
illustrated by Ross Collins

Cinderella
Written by Barrie Wade,
illustrated by Julie Monks

The Three Little Pigs
Written by Maggie Moore,
illustrated by Rob Hefferan

Jack and the Beanstalk
Written by Maggie Moore,
illustrated by Steve Cox

The Three Billy Goats Gruff
Written by Barrie Wade,
illustrated by Nicola Evans

Goldilocks and the Three Bears
Written by Barrie Wade,
illustrated by Kristina Stephenson

Little Red Riding Hood
Written by Maggie Moore,
illustrated by Paula Knight

Rapunzel
Written by Hilary Robinson,
illustrated by Martin Impey

Snow White
Written by Anne Cassidy,
illustrated by Melanie Sharp

The Emperor's New Clothes
Written by Karen Wallace,
illustrated by François Hall

The Pied Piper of Hamelin
Written by Anne Adeney,
illustrated by Jan Lewis

Hansel and Gretel
Written by Penny Dolan,
illustrated by Graham Philpot

The Sleeping Beauty
Written by Margaret Nash,
illustrated by Barbara Vagnozzi